HALFTIME

Halftime

KIM FINDLAY

HeartEyes
Press

To the Pitsquirrels
Couldn't have done this without you.

PROLOGUE

Faith

One year ago

A phone call at 3 a.m. is guaranteed to mess up your life.

I was sound asleep, tired the way only a day spent doing nothing in a hospital waiting room can make you. My grandmother had had a stroke. We'd come home at 10 p.m. when the doctors told us they were cautiously optimistic and that we should get some sleep.

I don't usually answer unknown numbers—*Hello? Text?*—and when I pulled up out of some weird dream, I thought it was the hospital calling. I'd already accepted the call when I remembered they had my parents' numbers, not mine.

"I'm so, so sorry. So sorry, babe. It's not my— I'm just— I'm so sorry…"

I went from sleepy to wide awake and suspicious in about two seconds. I knew that voice. I didn't know why he was calling from someone else's phone, but that was my boyfriend's voice.

His drunk voice.

Apologizing.

I hadn't seen him in two weeks, not since he left for college and I started my senior year in high school. I don't know what anyone else would think getting a drunken apology call at 3 a.m. from their boyfriend, but growing up in my family? I gripped my phone tightly, because I was pretty sure I was about to hear he'd been kissing someone else.

"Seb." I didn't say anything else. My heart was pounding like I was facing a breakaway on the ice. My focus sharpened, and I put up my blocker, ready to protect my net. Or, in this case, I put up my emotional blocker to stop the hurt I could sense coming.

"Babe, I'm so sorry. It wasn't on purpose, I promise. I'm so, so sorry."

He was crying. This was going to be bad. I bit down on my lip to stop it from quivering.

"I thought it was— I mean, I was so out of it."

I'd told him a long-distance relationship was not going to work. He'd said we could do it. He'd promised.

He'd *promised*.

He knew what my parents were like. He'd promised he could be faithful. But if he'd kissed another girl, I didn't think I could take it.

"Seb, what did you do? Did you kiss someone?"

"I didn't know— I thought it was you..."

That sounded sincere, but what did I know? My mother had believed my father, too.

"What happened, Seb?"

I'd spent a shittastic day waiting to find out if my grandmother was going to die, and I was tired and low on patience.

I heard him snuffle. "I was in bed, and then—" I couldn't make out his next words, but dread was numbing me, "—she didn't taste right and...a condom—"

I cut the connection before he could say another word. I'd considered what I'd do if he'd kissed someone else. Sex of any kind? I would not EVER forgive that.

My blocker was up, my pads keeping all emotion at bay. I blocked the number that had just called me as it rang through again. Then I blocked Seb's number. I blocked him on every social-media platform I had. Then I turned off my phone and threw it at the wall.

The pain hit hard. I had no mental shields, none that could protect against this.

He'd cheated. He'd known what that would do to me—he'd *known*—and he'd called drunk and wanting to apologize for that? I wrapped my arms around my knees and gripped as hard as I could. It didn't help. As a lump pushed up in my throat, my eyes started to water, and I promised myself that I was not my mother. I was not EVER going to be with a cheater. I'd rather spend my life alone.

Fuck Sebastien. Oh wait, someone already did.

1

Sebastien

Sophomore year is going to be so much better than freshman year. For starters, I'm entering the arena at Burlington University to watch the freshmen at their first on-ice practice. Last year, I was in the locker room sweating my balls off, wondering if I was going to make it or not.

I mean, I knew I *should* make it. I'd done well on my Junior A team back in Canada before earning a scholarship here, but sometimes my nerves got the best of me. When I was in a new situation, I was always afraid I wouldn't be wanted.

This year, I wasn't new. I spotted a bunch of the guys sitting a few rows up, so I headed to join them. I felt my phone buzz and pulled it out of my pocket as I climbed the steps. I smiled when I saw it was my girlfriend texting me a photo.

That's another thing that's going to be better than last year. This time last year, I didn't know it, but I was about to lose my girlfriend. Faith had been a senior in high school. She'd wanted to break up when I left for college, but I'd convinced her long distance would work.

Long story short, it didn't.

This year, it's different. Holly and I started going out the end

5

of our freshman year, and being a lot smarter, we took a break over the summer. We reconnected a few days ago and decided to get back together.

Much better way to handle things. I'm learning.

I sat down beside my teammates, still looking at the photos Holly sent me, and got some teasing from the guys. That was the other thing that was so much better this year. I knew these guys. After a year together, we'd bonded. We were family. I didn't have any other family worth talking about.

"Is that Holly texting you?" Cooper, a junior defenseman, asked. He'd adopted me last year after the big breakup with my girlfriend. I'd needed somebody then, and he'd come through, in aces. I owed him.

I nodded, flipping between two photos Holly had sent me. She wanted to know which I liked better. Hell if I knew. I mean, the photos weren't that clear, and she looked good in both of them.

"What's she sending you photos for when she's not naked?" Cooper leaned over my shoulder to look at the photos. I elbowed him. Cooper's a player, the off-ice kind, so not really a guy to ask for advice on relationships.

"She wants to know which one I like."

He shrugged. "Whichever one shows more skin."

I shook my head, then took another look at the photos. Maybe he had a point.

Next thing, Holly sent me two more photos, and I was looking for a way to bail. I wasn't Dr. Phil, but I could see a lot of ways this could go bad if I picked the wrong one.

I heard a whistle from Forts, our captain, and looked up. Our freshmen weren't on the ice yet. The women had first dibs on the ice today. I didn't pay a lot of attention to the women's team, because my ex, the one that broke up with me last September, played hockey. Nothing against the Moo U women hockey players, but I didn't need the reminder.

The guys were watching one of the goalies on the ice. The women had wrapped up most of their practice, best I could tell, and were just shooting at the net. And the one player? The goalie?

Damn, she was good.

Really good.

Déjà vu good.

I didn't know how to describe what was happening to me. My cheeks were warm, but my body was cold. My stomach was ready to hurl my lunch, and an unseen weight pressed down on me.

And through it all, I couldn't take my eyes off her.

I knew it was her without seeing the face hidden behind the mask or the name on the back of her jersey. I knew those moves, the way she slid across the crease, the quick flick of her blocker to deflect a shot. She was even better than she'd been a year ago. No wonder the guys were watching her. She didn't play like a freshman goalie. She was confident and focused and…

And she hated me.

"Who's that?" I heard Cooper say, and there was no doubt who he was talking about. There were six of us sitting there, and all six of us were watching her.

Just her.

"Dev." I heard my mouth speaking but had no memory of making it happen. "Her jersey says Devereaux, right?"

I figured it out. I was dreaming. That was why I felt so weird. That was why my mouth was spitting out words when I hadn't given it permission to. It was some weird dream, probably connected to this being close to the anniversary of our breakup. I waited it out, knowing I'd wake up long before I had to see her face. Sure, this dream felt almost real, but it couldn't be, because Faith would never come to Burlington, not when she knew I was here.

Of course not.

The coach blew her whistle, and the goalie turned around, Devereaux written across the back of her jersey. Number thirty-one. Faith's number.

Because in my dream, I hadn't changed anything.

7

"Shit, Seb, you know her?"

Dream Cooper was surprised by this, as apparently were the rest of the guys on the team. But it was okay, I'd wake up soon.

"Yeah, she played in the same town as I did as a Junior." Fortunately, dream me was smart enough not to say I knew her, as in *naked* knew her. Did not want to talk about that.

Instead, dream me rattled on about something else. "First practice on the Mav's, we all tried to score on her. I think about two shots got in out of at least a hundred. She's good."

Dream Cooper got a glint in his eye, and I knew he was about to get up to some stupid shit. Cooper was the biggest contributor to our kitty. We threw in money when we did something we shouldn't and gave it to a charity at the end of the year. Good thing this was just a dream.

"Really?" Dream Cooper wasn't giving up on the idea. Real Cooper was just the same.

"Yeah, she played on the guys' teams until she wasn't allowed to anymore."

Cooper turned to the rest of my dream teammates and said, "Let's go guys. The freshmen need to see if they can do better than Seb's sorry-ass Junior team."

They all agreed, got up, and headed down to the ice. Dream me stayed put, waiting to wake up. It was definitely time for this to be over. My phone buzzed again, and I saw Holly had sent more pictures. I looked at them, wondering why I was so interested in women's fashion in a dream. And it had to be a dream, right?

I shook my head. Down by the ice, Cooper called Faith. She skated over and tugged off her helmet. Sweaty hair surrounded her face, and the long blond braid fell down her shoulder. She pulled her arm over her forehead, wiping off the sweat. Like she did every damn time. And the bubble I'd created by telling myself this was a dream popped.

My hands started to shake. The phone buzzed again, but now I felt like I really was about to hurl. I found my feet and headed away from the ice, away from my teammates, away from *her*. I came to in the hallway, leaning against the wall like I'd fall down if I tried to stand up straight. I breathed in and out, concentrating on keeping my food inside me.

What the everlasting fuck?

Faith was here? Why the hell would she be here? She knew this was where I'd gotten a scholarship. This was my school.

Shit. Sophomore year had just gone to shit.

Faith

Not every day was a good day. Some days, I couldn't stop a beachball coming at my net. I didn't have many of those days. I was good. So good that I'd been offered scholarships to a lot of schools. I'd had choices. My dad and I had gone over all of them, making up a pro and con list. The biggest pro was getting ice time.

I was a goalie. When my team was on the ice, there were five skaters and one goaltender. A team would normally run four forward lines and three pair of defensemen every game. That meant eighteen or more skaters would play in a game, and only one goalie. The backup goalie would only come in if the starter let in a slew of goals or got hurt. Bottom line? There weren't a lot of goalies on a team's roster, and they didn't all get to play.

It was important that I had the chance to be in net for games. I was going to play hockey professionally, so I needed to show what I could do while I was at college. Dad and I looked at a lot more than team records and facilities. We checked out what the rosters were like, how deep they were with goalies both playing and ready to play.

The best shot to play was at Burlington University, known as Moo U. Moo U's starting goalie had graduated last year. Her backup, Claire Anderson, was a rising senior, and this was her last year playing. They didn't have any other goalies ready to start. Of course, the biggest con about Burlington was my ex. I knew he must be playing here this year, that is unless my darkest wishes had come true and he'd lost a leg or something. I'd been careful not to hear or see anything about him.

Bitter much? Yeah, I was.

I couldn't tell my dad I didn't want to go to Burlington because my ex had cheated on me. That wasn't a topic we discussed in our house.

And hell, I wasn't going to let my ex decide my future. I needed to put my hockey career first. That meant ignoring anything to do with him and taking care of myself. I'd been ignoring him for a year. I could keep it up. So I'd taken the offer from Burlington.

I'd been here on campus for a couple of days now. I was learning my way around, getting to know my roommate, and had seen no signs of my ex. So far, so good.

Today was our first practice. It was just the freshmen on the ice, though I had noticed some people sitting watching us. I knew some of them had to be some of my upper-class teammates. I was looking forward to meeting them, but first I needed to impress them with my skills.

If I could show them I was the goalie they needed, they'd be predisposed to like me.

Women playing hockey did not get all the perks and advantages that the guys got. We had to play for the love of the game, and we were all fiercely competitive. We had to be, or we'd all give up.

Fortunately, I was having one of my best days. First, we did some drills. Most of those were for the skaters. We goalies had different needs and did a lot of exercises and practice on our own. There was another freshman goalie here, but it soon became blindingly obvious I was better. I had to be. If I was going to be a professional, I had to be better than everyone. Because I didn't want to play with women. I wanted to play with men.

My favorite part of the rookie exhibition was at the end, when the skaters took shots, and the other goalie and I did our best to stop them. This was what I lived for. And today everything was going well. The puck had slowed down, and I saw everything coming. I knew it would be harder with the rest of the team, with the better, more-experienced players, but for now, I let my mind go into my zone.

There was nothing but me and the puck. It was a battle I'd been fighting as long as I could remember. And today I was winning.

The whistle blew, and the shots stopped coming. I stood straight, flipped up my visor, and turned to suck some water through the straw in one of the bottles I'd left on the net. I was coming back to reality now, my body coated in sweat, my muscles vibrating from released tension. This was the closest I'd been to a game in weeks, and I was buzzing, still ready to go. The rest of the players had already started toward the locker rooms. I gathered my stuff and started to follow them when I heard someone shouting my name.

"Devereaux!"

I hadn't expected someone to call me out like that. My coach had called on me during practice, but this was a male voice, not Coach Cray's. I hadn't been here at school long enough to get to know anyone not connected with my team. Maybe it was bizarre, but I only knew women on campus so far.

It was definitely me they were calling though. There were five guys down near the ice, and it wasn't hard to figure out they were hockey players. They were big and fit, built the way they needed to be to play my sport. Plus, they had that air of confidence that the men's teams swaggered around with. Moo U didn't have a football team, and the hockey team was the jock royalty on campus. The men's hockey team, of course. My roommate had already checked them out and told me more than enough about them. I knew the rookies for the men's team were next on the ice, so these guys were obviously here to check out the new blood, just like the women had been here to watch me.

Not gonna lie, for a minute, I checked every face, making sure none of them were my ex. I hated that I reacted that way, but I hadn't completely gotten over him. At least, not to the point of not caring about him. Maybe I should break my own rule and check whether he was still here, or if he'd managed to get dengue fever. Or leprosy. When none of the faces were familiar, I relaxed and skated over to see what these guys wanted.

I tugged off my helmet. I knew my face would be flushed and my hair would be sticking to me with sweat, but I didn't let that bother me. I had no romantic interest in any of them. I'd promised myself not to date an athlete and gone against that once. I wouldn't again. I shook out my hair, wiped my face, and waited to hear what they wanted. Best case, they'd tell me I'd played well, because damn it, I had. Worst case, smack talk. I could handle both.

"Hello, ladies. How can I help you?"

I might as well start the ball rolling. I'd played with boys before. I didn't need them to like me, but I did need them to respect me. And in the locker room, trash talking could earn respect.

"Cute," said a tall blond. He appeared to be the leader of the group, and I took note. He was leaning against the boards, confidence oozing out his pores. That was fine. I was just as confident.

"I hear you think you're pretty good."

I could work with this. I shook my head. "Nah, I *know* I'm *great*." I gave them my widest smile.

Blondie smirked. One of the other guys looked shocked. I focused on Blondie.

"I also hear you think you can take on men."

A snort from behind him let me know they'd caught Blondie's double entendre. Again, nothing I hadn't handled before. It was a challenge to see what I could take.

"Are you asking me for a date, Blondie, or do you want to play hockey?"

He ran his gaze over me, so I did the same to him. He wasn't going to see much. I was covered with pads. I could verify that he was fit and had money to spend on clothes, but the appraisal was a gesture, not interest on my part.

No athletes. Especially not hockey players. Assuming any offered.

Blondie crossed his arms and cocked his head. "Think any of these freshman or rookies can score on you?"

A couple of guys had made it onto the ice. I was the only one from the women's team still around.

I ignored the look on his face, the smirky do-you-get-what-I'm-suggesting look.

"They won't be able to get the puck past me, unless they're very, very lucky. And I don't think any of them are that lucky today."

A big grin creased his face. "Okay, then let's do it."

I blinked. "Seriously?"

He stood up. "Unless you're just talk?"

I jerked my head at the male coach who'd just stepped onto the ice. "If he's okay with it, then bring it."

Blondie called out, and the coach skated over. Not hard to see that Blondie had some clout on the men's team. I wondered if he was a senior or junior.

"Hey, Coach Garfunkle. Can we have a little fun here? Devereaux here is pretty good. Maybe the new guys can give her some more practice and see if they can get the puck past her?"

I thought there was a good chance the coach would blow off the idea immediately, but instead, he looked at Blondie, then at me, and then stared out over the ice at who knew what.

"Sure, Coop." He nodded. "We've got a few minutes before we need to get started here."

I took another gulp of water before putting my helmet back on. "Watch and learn, ladies!" I taunted as I skated back to the net.

I could talk a good game with any of the teammates I'd had, boy or girl, and the ones I'd played against. That was part of the whole scenario. But unless it was a bad day, I could back it up.

And today was a good day. These guys, dressed for the first time as the Moo U team, were anxious to look good for their coach and teammates. They'd brought their A game. But I had an A-plus game going.

It's not that no one could score—but almost no one did. I wasn't perfect even on my best day, but only two pucks got past me, and one of those bounced off the post, hit my back, and went in. On more than fifty shots, that was acceptable.

I still wanted the other one back.

As much fun as it was, they did have a practice to run, so the coach whistled, the guys gathered around him, and I was left alone in the net. Again, I gathered up my stuff, pulled off the helmet, and prepared to skate over to the women's locker room.

"Devereaux!" It was Blondie, Coop. "Not too shabby."

I pulled my hand out of my glove and scratched my nose with my middle finger. I heard the guys laugh, and I skated off the ice with a smile.

Fifteen minutes later, I was in my coach's office, and I wasn't smiling.

"Why are you here, Ms. Devereaux?"

I'd been told to stop and see her before I left. I wasn't sure what was up, but I'd knocked on her door as soon as I'd showered. No one wants to be on their coach's bad side. She told me to come in and then glared at me. Apparently, she hadn't asked to see me to say I'd done a good job in practice.

I wasn't sure what answer she was looking for, so I went with my honest response. "I'm here to play hockey."

She leaned back in her chair with her arms crossed. "With which team?"

Oh shit. I could only give one answer. "The women's team." *Obviously.*

"Then why were you on the ice with the men?"

I didn't know this woman yet. I didn't know if she had a sense of humor. I didn't know if I was totally screwed. "It was a kind of joke."

"A joke? Do you think our team here is a joke?"

Shit. Shit. Shit. "No, ma'am. It was something the Junior team did back home, a thing for the rookies. To show them that a woman could stop them, so they didn't think—"

"I don't know or care what you did 'back home'. I'm worried about what you do here. I don't need one of my players being a 'joke' for the men's team. Maybe it's different 'back home', but here, we've had to fight for everything we have in the women's hockey program. I don't need to lose ground because a freshman wants some attention from the boys."

My mouth dropped open. *Attention from the boys?* Did she think I was desperate for them to like me? "With all due respect, ma'am, I didn't want their attention. I wanted them to know that a woman can be just as good at hockey as they are."

Coach's eyes snapped with anger, and she leaned forward, an angry expression on her face. "Just as good at hockey? I don't need an overconfident freshman on a mission to show the world she's just as good at hockey as the men. I need team players, players who want to be here, who want to play *women's* hockey. Yes, Ms. Devereaux, I know you've played with the boys. And I know who your father is. And I don't give a flying…fig. If you're playing here only because there isn't a 'boys' team that will sign you, you can pack your duffle and go. I have no room for divas and egos on this team. You're good, Ms. Deveraux, but if you're not a team player, you're no good to me. If you come back to our next practice, I expect a better attitude. Think it over. And close the door on your way out."

Fuck. Fuck, fuck, fuck, fuck, fuck.

By the time Coach was done ripping me a new one, the rest of my teammates were gone. I packed up to leave, feeling like I'd just tanked my entire future.

Fuck!

I wondered how she'd found out I was playing with the guys. I wondered if one of my teammates had seen me and told her. Did the whole team hate me now, or just my coach? How could I fix this? When I'd had trouble with teammates before, there'd been an easy solution. Play better. Because when a team was winning games, everything tended to go more smoothly. But now, if I played well, was everyone going to think I was just doing it to show the guys I was as good as they were? Because I wished I was playing with them?

Truthfully, to reach my goals, I couldn't be as good as the guys, I had to be better. And I couldn't do that unless I played.

Fuck.

I wished I had someone to talk to, but I didn't know my teammates yet, and they might already hate me. Obviously, talking to my coach was out. I wasn't calling my parents. I didn't need my dad interfering. I slammed out of the locker room, mood a complete 180 from when I'd left the ice a half hour ago. I was blinking back tears, because I could not be the emotional girl as well as the show-off.

I was tired and upset and angry and ready for this day to be over already. I wasn't looking where I was going and ran into someone. A tall, hard, masculine someone, because it was just that perfect a day. I muttered sorry and stepped to the side, wanting nothing more than to get to my room where I didn't have to worry about anyone seeing me while I tried to come to grips with what had just happened.

"Faith?"

I froze. This could not be happening, not today. Did I torture some orphans in a past life, or kill kittens? I knew that voice. It belonged to the one person I didn't want to see ever again.

"Faith?" He said it again, so staring at the ground was apparently not going to make either of us disappear.

I drew in a long breath and slowly raised my head.

It was him. Seb, the cheater. He looked shocked, like I was the last person he'd expected to see.

2

Sebastien

I couldn't believe it.

Yes, I'd seen her on the ice. So, yeah, I knew she was here. But not like *here*. Not standing in front of me. I had no idea what to do, so I stood looking like an idiot for long enough that a custodian brushed by, upsetting my balance. I tilted in, almost falling against her, and raised my arms to catch my weight on my hands, effectively caging her against the wall.

She was right here.

I'd forgotten how nice it was to have a girl's face so close to mine. Faith wasn't much shorter than I was, so I'd never had to hunch over to kiss her. My eyes went straight to her lips.

Déjà vu.

How many times had I stood in front of her like this, watching those lips so often chapped from time in the arena? Her tongue slipped out, dragged over her bottom lip. My signal to...

I looked up at her eyes, wanting to see what she was feeling. She'd been surprised. I'd seen that, but now her eyes were wide with something else. Something so familiar. It was like this past year had never happened. Like I'd just left Canada a few days ago. That same damn look that told me if I didn't kiss her soon, she'd pull my head down to kiss me instead.

I was moving, leaning toward her, looking at her lips again, when a loud sound broke the spell.

My phone.

I jerked back, and Faith ducked under my arm. I reached into my pocket, muscle memory moving my hand as my brain scrambled the thoughts of Faith and her kiss. She wasn't looking at me anymore. I could see the flush on her cheeks, but her head was down, and she was walking away. I must have swiped the phone without thinking. I heard a voice, tinny and small since the phone was down near my hip, not at my ear.

"Sebastien? Seb? Are you there?"

Holly.

Shit. What did I think I was doing? I had a girlfriend.

I quickly lifted the phone to my ear. "Yeah, Holly, I'm here."

I didn't catch the first couple of sentences she said. I was watching the back of Faith as she pushed out the nearest doors.

"Sorry, Holly. What was that again?"

She wanted to go out to dinner with her friend and her friend's boyfriend tonight. I agreed. I felt guilty because of whatever had just happened with Faith. We were over, as over as you could get, so I had no idea what to do with that moment. But also, there was a party tonight at the hockey house, where I lived with some of the team. I was pretty sure the guys had said they'd invited the women's team to come.

I was not ready to see Faith again. Not until I got my head wrapped around her being here at Burlington. Not until I figured out why she was here, and how I felt about it. Because despite what had happened just now, she'd cut me off twelve months ago and not reached out again. It was safe to say that she'd broken up with me, and that hadn't changed.

I loved living at the hockey house. It wasn't the most luxurious place, and honestly, it needed a good clean a lot of the time, but we were all teammates, and while I was in school, this was my home. I visited my parents, but I didn't have a home with them. I didn't even have my own room.

I understood that they'd married because they'd gotten pregnant with me, and it hadn't worked out. Then they'd remarried and started new families. Families that did work out. I was...the prototype that didn't take.

It was different with the team. I fit here. I had my own room. Last year, I'd been up on the third floor where it was freezing in winter, hot when summer hit, and small with crooked ceilings all the time. This year, I'd managed dibs on a room on the second floor, so I no longer bumped my head on the ceiling.

I told Holly I'd pick her up early for our double date. She liked that. Things had been a little hectic so far, settling in and catching up with people, so she was happy we could have some time together. I still felt a little guilty. Because not only had I almost kissed Faith this afternoon, I'd suggested we meet up early because I wanted out of the house to make sure I wouldn't run into Faith again.

I debated whether I should tell Holly about Faith. She knew a little of the story. We'd broken up before the summer because of what had happened between Faith and me last year, so she knew that I'd tried long distance with an ex, the ex thought I'd cheated and cut off all contact. I'd told her I didn't think long distance was good for us over the summer, especially since we hadn't been dating very long. I wasn't sure if I should tell her that my ex was now at school here. I didn't want her to worry. I did know I shouldn't tell her I'd almost kissed Faith. I'd thought that over, and it wasn't going to happen again.

I put it down to just the shock of being suddenly that close to Faith without warning. We hadn't had what you'd call closure. The end of us had been a disaster, and I obviously hadn't dealt with it, not properly. But it wasn't going to be a shock to see her again. I knew she was here. And I knew Faith. She wasn't going to be kissing me, either.

"What's up, Hunts?"

Cooper was in the doorway of my room, hands stretched up to grab the lintel. His room was across the hall. He was another defenseman on the team, but I'd never had the chance to play with him. Last year, Cooper had been out all season with an injury. He'd been nice enough to spend time with me, helping me navigate and giving me some good advice, about hockey and life, and we got along well. I was hoping we'd play together this year.

"I'm picking up Holly."

"For the party?"

I shrugged. "Nah, I'm missing this one. We're going out for dinner. Catching up."

Coop rolled his eyes. "Hunts, I give up on you. It's the first party of the year, we've got freshmen girls coming, and you're back with the girlfriend?"

I shrugged again. We'd debated this last year. I liked to be in a relationship, and Cooper liked one and done. We're different like that. On the ice, I was a stay-at-home defenseman, protecting our net, while he was more of an offensive threat. It reflected our personalities. We were opposite enough to get along off the ice, and I thought that would work on the ice as well.

For tonight though, the freshmen were all his. Even Faith. If she came. No, Faith wouldn't be interested in someone like Cooper, a player. But if Faith was coming, I needed to be gone.

"Less competition for you."

Cooper wasn't worried. He was much better looking than I was, so he never had a problem attracting attention.

"Are you and Holly coming to the party after?"

I froze. Should I? I didn't want to. Not if Faith was going to be here. I just… I didn't know how we were going to act around each other. Obviously, we weren't going to almost kiss again, but would she acknowledge me? Admit we were exes? Could we be friends?

No, not friends.

But until I knew how it was going down, I wasn't adding Holly to the mix.

I shook my head. "We're going out with her best friend and her boyfriend. Maybe the next one."

Because my roommates loved to party, and since the legal drinking age in Vermont was twenty-one, we couldn't drink in bars. Not us lower classmen. Most of the time, we went to the Biscuit in the Basket after games, but then a lot of us couldn't have beer. So we had parties to handle that particular need. Lots of parties.

"Okay then. You go play happy families while we have fun."

I made sure my smile stayed in place. I wasn't trying to play happy families. I didn't have a good experience with families, but there was no need to share that. Instead, I checked that I had my phone and wallet and keys and went to meet my girlfriend. Parties were fun, but having someone who was there for you? Miles better.

Faith

"You promised!" my roommate Penny whined.

I'd made the mistake of telling her I'd been invited to a party at the hockey house. I'd had no idea she'd flip out about it. Apparently, being invited to one of the hockey houses was a big deal.

How did she know this? We were both freshmen.

While I'd done all kinds of research on the women's hockey team and what happened on the ice, Penny had been researching the men's team and the extracurricular stuff.

The male hockey players were at the top of the totem pole at Moo U. That explained a lot. Why Coach Cray was so upset with me. Why Penny had talked me into letting her go to the party with me tonight. Why things had gone the way they had with Seb a year ago. Then today, the way I'd responded, like we were still—

Nope, not going there. I was blocking everything connected to him, closing it up in a box and locking it. What happened today was buried in that box. But that didn't mean I wanted to go to a party where I'd run into him. For all I knew, he could be living at this hockey house. He'd definitely been staying somewhere other than res last year. At least, that's where he'd started, back when we were— Nope.

I was not facing him again. Especially not with *Holly*. I'd be willing to bet Holly was his girlfriend. Or a girlfriend. Or had been his hookup. Maybe even the one from last year...

Damn it all. I was not going to dwell on that, or have my life screwed up thinking about Seb.

"Come on, Faith. You said we could go. You said your teammates were gonna be there, so you had to show."

Yeah, I had said all that. Damn it. I wanted to hang out with my teammates. Especially after the thing on the ice today. I didn't want them to think, like Coach did, that I didn't want to be part of the team. That I thought I was too good for them or only wanted to play with the guys.

There was a chance that Seb wouldn't be there. If he was... Well, it was a party, right? According to Penny, the hockey parties were the best parties on campus. That meant a lot of people. I could avoid Seb, couldn't I? I absolutely could.

"You're right, we should go."

Penny actually bounced with excitement. She looked like a little copper-haired Yorkie high on sugar and dancing around the room at the chance to go for a walk.

Penny and I were roommates because we were both freshies and had both signed up for the Wellness Environment, or WE residence. I'd wanted to be here because I already was on a special diet for the hockey team. This was the "healthy" res, and my main goal was getting ice time. Eating healthily, without a lot of temptations, was a no brainer.

Penny was in the dorm so she wouldn't get fat. Her words. She was this tiny pixie of a thing, and I was an elephant next to her. She was five foot nothing, and I guessed a size zero or two. I was just half an inch under six feet and a hockey player. I felt… not very feminine around her. I'd always been the tall, big girl in my classes. I shoved my phone in the back pocket of my jeans and my keys in the front.

"Ready?"

Penny was staring at me. "Are you not going to change? Or anything?"

I looked down at myself, as if I didn't know what I had on. This is what I wore. Jeans. Not skirts or dresses, because my legs were thick and muscled and not slender. I didn't show my upper arms and shoulders because they were muscled, too.

Penny's eyes went wide. "I'm so sorry. I mean, if you want to cover yourself or hide…or something like that. I mean, you don't have to tell me if anything happened to you. Just, um, forget what I said." She plastered this crazy grin on her face.

Shit. I didn't need her to think I was wounded or damaged or something.

"Penny, I'm fine. I'm just not a girlie girl, so I'm not going to dress up."

Penny blinked at me. Had there been something in my tone? "A girlie girl? What's that supposed to mean?" She sounded upset, and I hadn't meant to do that. Or maybe I had. Because the differences between the two of us were obvious.

"I'm not like you. Tiny and pretty and girlie."

"Are you serious? I mean, really serious with that shit?"

Okay, she was definitely pissed. I waved a hand at her. "Like you can't see how different we are?"

She had her hands on her hips and looked like a pissed-off pixie. "I know I'm short, thanks very much. And I don't like to sweat, so I'm not in super shape like you. But that doesn't mean I'm 'girlie'. Are you saying girls can't have muscles? Can't be tall? What exactly is your problem?"

How did I explain this without making her even more upset?

"It's just that you look like girls in magazines and movies. I don't."

Penny shook a finger in my face. "I don't know who did this to you, but you are just as girlie as you want to be, whether you look like you or like me. I've seen some of the women hockey players here. They wear makeup and pretty dresses, so don't tell me you can't dress up if you want."

I hadn't seen any of my teammates except at practice so far, and none of them wore makeup then. I mean, it would be sweat off halfway through. And no one had pretty dresses at practice. Tonight was my first chance to hang out with them out of the arena or weight room. Maybe things were different here. Maybe jeans and a T-shirt weren't going to cut it.

"When did you see the women's team?"

Pixie girl rolled her eyes at me. "I did research! I looked at their Insta accounts and school media pictures. I didn't just look at the guys."

I'd narrowed my research to hockey on the ice. Maybe this wasn't like my team back home. Maybe they'd all be dressed up, and I'd look stupid if I showed up like this. I didn't need any more marks against me.

I glanced over at Penny. She still had her hands on her hips. I sighed. "I don't know how to be a girlie girl."

Just like that, the anger was gone. She came over and patted my arm. "Oh, sweetie, I can help."

For a moment, I worried. I had no idea what this girl might do to me. Then I remembered Seb. Seb and his probable girlfriend. I was sure she knew how to dress and look pretty. Suddenly, I wanted to look good. Like a girlie girl. Like someone he didn't know.

I put myself in Penny's hands.

Penny was discouraged at the start. Sharing clothes was obviously never going to happen, but she went through my wardrobe to find what she thought was the best outfit for the party. She muttered under her breath about a lot of my stuff, but she did finally find something she could live with. My mother must have bought and packed the skirt, because I swear, I don't remember seeing it before.

I thought my legs looked...too bulky. Too muscled. Penny shook her finger at me again and told me to stop being stupid. The tank top was plain, but she dug into her own jewelry box to find some dangly necklaces. She didn't like the little bit of makeup I had, but she did her best with me. I only had flat sandals, and that passed her approval. Even in flats, I was taller than a lot of guys. I always wore my hair either in a ponytail or braid. I was used to long hair, and I liked the way my helmet fit with it. I pulled it back, but Penny told me my hair was gorgeous and insisted I wear it down.

When I looked in the mirror and saw the skirt, my arms and legs showing, my hair falling down over my shoulders, I almost didn't recognize myself. I still thought I looked like a giant beside Penny, but not a hideous one. I decided I didn't look too bad.

Penny frowned when I said that, but this was the happiest I'd felt about going out since... I don't know. Elementary school sleepovers. I was grateful to her. That made her smile, and we headed out for the hockey house. It wasn't hard to find the place. The campus wasn't huge, and the party had definitely started. The windows were open, the music was loud, and there were lots of people spilling out onto the porch.

I should have been looking for some of my teammates first. After the run-in with Coach Cray, I wanted to be sure they understood I wanted to be part of the team. But before I looked for them, I looked for Seb. I needed to know where to avoid. If I could miss interacting with him again, I might just have some fun at this party.

I couldn't see Seb, which made me a little nervous. But Penny dragged me in to find something to drink, so I followed her, eyes watching the crowd. No Seb. It occurred to me that he might not want to see me again, either. He should feel bad. He was the guilty one. With that assurance, and a solo cup of beer in my hand, I was ready to have fun. I told Penny I needed to look for my teammates. She was looking for hot hockey players of the male persuasion, so we promised to check in later and split up.

I was grateful to Penny as I moved through the crowd. I didn't see any other women in jeans and T-shirts, so dressing up was a thing here. I felt too tall and too big around a lot of the girls, but I could hear Penny's voice yelling at me when those thoughts came in. I heard a group of girls laughing, spun around to see if it was my team, and almost spilled beer over a guy. He looked familiar, but it took me a minute. It was Blondie from the rink.

I felt the smile on my face. Yeah, I'd gotten in shit, but it wasn't this guy's fault. And I knew I'd played well. Those guys might not want to admit it, but they had to be impressed.

He cocked his head, hair falling over his forehead. "Do I know you? Did we hook up or something?"

Well, he was obviously a player, and I didn't mean on the ice. I didn't care about that because I wasn't interested in him, or any of the other hockey guys, not in that way. But I was interested in hockey.

"You've already forgotten who shut down your freshmen this afternoon?" I saw the recognition hit, and his gaze ran down my body. Once he was looking at my face again, I made a circling motion with my hand.

"What?"

"My turn. I want to objectify you now."

He grinned and turned, hands held high to keep his cup of beer safe. "Well?"

I shook my head. "Sorry. Not my type."

He laughed, and I saw some of the girls in the room watching, a few with unhappy expressions. I got it. He was good looking, tall and well built, and a hockey player. On this campus, that probably got him anything he wanted. Wasn't going to get anything from me though.

"Come over and meet some of the guys." He put his hand on my back, ready to direct me. I decided that armed with his admiration and a cup of cheap beer, I could face Seb if I needed to.

I didn't.

There were a handful of guys around a foosball game, a couple of whom I thought I'd seen at the rink. None were my ex. Blondie, whose name was Cooper, introduced me to the guys as the goalie who'd stopped the freshmen.

They asked about where I'd played and trained, which led to discussing where they'd done the same. That led to talk about the hockey at college level and pro, too. I was into that. I was surprised so many of the guys were willing to stand talking hockey when I could see there were women around ready to spend time with them.

Cooper was beside me for a lot longer than I'd expected. I wondered if he liked talking to me, or whether I'd become a challenge after I told him he wasn't my type. If so, he'd soon find out I wasn't joking.

My dad was a sports agent and a cheater. His clients were athletes, and enough of them were cheaters. I wasn't going there again. I'd made an exception for Seb, and he'd cheated, too. It just wasn't worth the hassle. Especially when my goal was to get playing time on my new team.

Shit.

I'd spent the whole night so far with these guys. It had been fun, but if Coach Cray found out, it would convince her I only wanted to be with the guys' team. I looked for Penny, using my height to my advantage, and finally found the copper-haired pixie on the stairs. I excused myself and headed that way.

Penny was talking to a couple of guys and saw me coming. She broke into a big smile. "Faith!" she yelled, voice incredibly loud considering it came out of such a petite body. I saw a lot of people turning her way.

"Faith, these guys are on the cross-country team!"

I nodded at them. They might be athletes, but I was focused on hockey, and not dating.

"Faith plays hockey!"

"Cool," the taller guy said.

It was obvious the shorter guy was interested in Penny. I knew my job. I kept the other guy distracted, letting Penny talk to her choice. Then I saw a girl I recognized from my team, Zoe, I think her name was. I excused myself, anxious to do some damage control with my teammates. Luckily, the team didn't seem to be bothered about what I'd done today. Zoe had seen me make Cooper twirl around and loved that. Points to me for bonding with a teammate. I heard more than I cared to about Cooper, and since I didn't want to talk about the players on the men's team, I turned the conversation back to our team. We had a lot we could talk about.

Penny tracked me down again. Her new friend couldn't stay late, since the cross-country guys had an early run the next morning. He'd offered to walk back to the dorm with Penny and me. I shot a glance at Penny, unsure if she wanted me along. Penny nodded, so I said good night to my teammates and headed out with Penny and her guy.

Cooper was with a group of people on the porch as we stepped outside, and he walked over to me. "Leaving?"

I nodded.

"Nice talking to you, Faith."

There was something weird about the way he said my name, but I didn't know why. Sure, it was kind of old-fashioned, but it wasn't the worst name out there.

Penny led the way down the sidewalk, followed by her new friend. I shot a glance back, and Cooper was watching me. Not the way he had when he'd given me the once over. His eyes were narrowed, and he wasn't smiling. I had no idea what he was up to, so I shrugged and followed my roommate.

The men's hockey team and the players on it were not my problem. In fact, it would probably be a good idea if I didn't spend any more time with them. That shouldn't be difficult. Since we shared a rink, we couldn't practice or play games at the same time. We had mornings on the ice, and they had the afternoons. On the weekends they had home games, we played away. Except for saying hi in passing, that should be it.

3

Sebastien

Holly looked good, and I made sure to tell her that. I couldn't remember if this was something she'd bought today and sent me a picture of, but she was pleased with the compliment, and we headed out to Tito's. I held her hand, and she happily told me about her day. She'd gone shopping and gotten her nails done. I was glad she'd had a good day. Hockey took up a lot of my time. When you added that to classes, it meant I was busy once the season got going. Holly and I had dated last year after the hockey season was over, so she didn't know what it was going to be like. Not yet.

Her friend and her date were already at Tito's when we arrived. We ordered drinks, and then Holly asked me about how practice went. I hadn't prepared for this. I didn't want to tell her about Faith being here. She knew Faith existed, knew she was the ex who'd broken up with me last year, but I hadn't told her a lot of details. Holly would freak, I was sure. Right now, I was trying to reassure her that we were together, that the summer apart hadn't been a bad thing.

The problem was that most of the freshman practice had been over by the time I gotten my shit together and joined my teammates. I didn't know if they'd say anything about Faith being in net during practice if the topic came up when Holly was around. They might say something since I'd missed a lot of the practice because I'd been freaking out about Faith being here.

The silence was becoming weird.

"Um, practice was fine. You know, freshmen still learning the ropes…"

The three were staring at me, but I didn't know what else to say. "Some of the guys looked good, a few were struggling. It will take time to find out what they're like."

"Was it your first practice?"

"This was just the freshmen. Not the rest of us. We're hitting the workout room tomorrow to get started, but we're not on the ice for another day." Holly and her friends weren't athletes, so they had no idea what this part of my life was like.

"Do you have to spend a lot of time doing that?"

Holly spoke for me. "Sebastien says they're super busy during the season. They practice or play every day but Sunday."

I'd described it to her, but it wasn't the same as living through it. "Sometimes, if it's an away game that's too far from here, we travel back on Sundays."

A frown creased Holly's brow. "You don't always even have Sundays?"

I shrugged. I really had told her what it was like.

"Isn't it hard to handle your classes and homework with all that?"

It was. That's why I'd warned Holly. I guess it hadn't sunk in. Holly blinked, and I wanted to swear. I'd *told* her.

"Hey, we can still make time, but it won't be as much as we want, not during the season. But the hockey house always puts on parties, and you're invited to all of those." I picked up her hand and dropped a kiss on it.

Her friend aahed, and Holly smiled. I relaxed, hoping she got it this time. I'd be busy, but I'd do what I could.

"Is your team good?" her friend's boyfriend asked. Holly had said he was some kind of computer major.

"We won the Frozen Four last year." I never knew how to answer questions like that. We were good, but I didn't want to sound like I was bragging. The next question was always about whether I was any good. How was I supposed to answer that? Yes, and I'm arrogant. No, and I'm either overly humble or useless to the team.

"Do you want to go pro?"

My knee was jiggling under the table, and I worked really hard to keep my voice even. "Isn't that everyone's dream?"

I hated that question, and I was going to get it a lot. This year, I was eligible for the hockey draft. Fortunately for me, our server arrived, and we concentrated on pizza toppings rather than my professional aspirations. The conversation moved on to some class the three of them were taking together, and I was able to sit back out of the spotlight, which I preferred.

I had to come up with an answer for that question, the one about going pro. This was the year I could declare for the draft. If I played like shit for the next couple of months, people would stop asking. But I didn't want to play like shit.

I loved hockey. This year, like every summer break from school, I'd been to hockey camps, and things had really started to click. There were no guarantees. I could hit the boards and be out for the season with an injury, like Coop had been last year. But unless something like that happened, I was looking at a good year. Really good. Declaring for the draft should be a given. Except, my parents didn't like that idea.

They liked a lot of things about hockey. They liked that I'd been able to attend camps whenever school was out. They loved when I was drafted for Juniors back in Canada and ended up with a team near Toronto. They loved that I'd stayed with a billet family. They loved when I got offers of scholarships to universities to play hockey. They weren't hurting for money, but they had other kids lined up after me that needed tuition money.

What my parents didn't like was the idea of me declaring for the draft, getting drafted, and dropping out of school to play, probably in some feeder league to see if I might get called up to play in the big league. They didn't like that an injury could leave me with no career and no education. And that could leave me their responsibility again.

I'd always been the outlier when it came to my family. If I got a degree and a normal job, maybe I'd fit in better. Fit in in a way I'd never done before. And honestly, the chances of ending up in the NHL were pretty small. The odds were getting better for me, but there were no guarantees.

I was torn, so mostly I tried to forget I had to make the decision soon. Until the season started and I found out how I was really playing, I could let it ride. Of course, ignoring it for now would be easier if people would just stop asking the question.

The rest of the date was fine. The pizza was good, and no one talked about hockey again. After we'd had our fill of pizza, and I'd passed on the cinnamon fritters—training was starting—we split the bill. Holly's friend lived in a different dorm, so we said goodbye to them and headed in the other direction.

Holly snuggled close to me. "I haven't seen your new room yet."

"We can't go to the hockey house," I said a little loudly.

Holly stopped in the street. "Why? You don't want me to see your room? Or your roommates?"

I took a breath. Holly was welcome to see my room, but I didn't want to go back there, not while there was a chance I'd see Faith. I wasn't ready for that yet. "They're having a party, so it's going to be a little crazy."

"They're having a party and you're not there?"

I could see Holly's insecurity building up again. It wasn't that I didn't want her at the party, or that I was ashamed for the guys to know we were going out again. I needed to go for a long run and work out this Faith stuff, ASAP.

"You asked if we could go out to dinner. And that sounded better than a noisy party with the freshies."

She was staring at my face as if she suspected me of lying. I wasn't. But I wasn't telling her everything. And that made me feel horrible.

"Next time, I'll take you to the party instead, but you'll probably regret it."

That must have reassured her, because she smiled and slipped her hand back into mine.

"Okay, Seb. I want you to tell me the things you want to do, too. Not always do what I plan."

"Sure." She didn't understand, not fully, how much I'd be limited by hockey commitments starting tomorrow. We might just as well do what she wanted while we could.

There were lots of students wandering around campus. Everyone was back for the fall semester now, but the big class assignments hadn't started yet, so no one was stressing about homework. I heard music and voices coming from every direction. Kids were partying while they could.

Burlington was a lot different from Toronto. And I loved it. I loved the feel of a smaller place. In Toronto, you missed a lot of the seasons, because the city was so built up. Here, you couldn't miss the leaves changing, the snow stayed white longer, and it smelled fresher.

Tonight, the air was soft, with just a hint of the cold weather coming.

We arrived at the doorway to Holly's dorm. I'd helped her move her stuff in, so I'd seen her room. She had a private bedroom. And she asked me to come up.

I was going to go up, and we'd have sex. That had become a given once I said my room wasn't available.

But...I couldn't.

Between Faith and the talk about the draft, I was too unsettled. I felt itchy, irritable. I needed that long run. Needed to put my mind in neutral for a while, let the pounding of my feet distract me from thinking, and see what nuggets of wisdom floated up from my subconscious.

"Sorry, Holly. I should go."

There was the worried look again. Damn it. What was my problem?

"You're going to the party?"

No, I wasn't going to go and try to party without her. But I wouldn't be able to focus on Holly the way she deserved if I went up there now, and I wasn't going to use her. I felt bad enough that I hadn't been completely with her mentally on our date.

"I want to get a run in before tomorrow. We're going to do weights and stuff, but I want to be sure my stamina is good."

That was a lie. I was in the best condition of my life. I felt bad about lying. But she'd feel worse if I told her I was going for a run because I wasn't sure how I felt about Faith being back. I needed to get that worked out immediately. Because it wasn't fair to Holly. And because I needed to get my life settled. This was a big year for me. I needed to get my shit together. I would. It might take ten miles or more, but I would.

Faith

I was a couple of weeks into my freshman year, and things were not working out the way I'd planned it.

I knew I'd have to deal with being on the same campus as Seb, and I could handle that. At least, I thought I could. Going forward, I would. As long as I wasn't suddenly shoved into his arms and unexpectedly caught up in those old feelings. We'd been together for almost two years. Lots of history. And that day at the rink was the first time I'd seen him since we'd broken up.

I was prepared now, focused on why we weren't together. I'd keep Seb at a distance and avoid him as much as possible. As much as I'd like to blame Seb for everything, I couldn't. It wasn't his fault Coach hated me. Or that I was struggling with classes. I was working my ass off in practices. I was the last one off the ice, and usually the first one on. I'd met all my teammates and done my best to get along. And honestly, I was playing really well. But Coach was convinced that everything I did was to impress the guys, and I had no idea how to change that.

Coach didn't do anything that crossed the line. She criticized, but legitimately. And she'd let me know when I did something impressive, but there was this look on her face, a tone in her voice, that told me she didn't buy it. Some of my teammates had noticed and asked what I'd done. By this point, they'd all heard about the shoot-out with the freshman guys. Most of them thought it was funny. I understood why Coach's ass was so bugged by it better now though. At Moo U, when people said hockey was king, they meant it. King. As in men. The women's team was an also-ran as far as things on campus went.

The big flyers around the school showed the men's team, not the women's. The photos in the university promo materials were all of the guys. The guys practiced in the afternoon, so we had to practice in the late morning, which made course selection a bitch. We shared the men's facilities, which were good, but only when the men weren't using them. After one of our training workouts was cancelled because of something the men's team needed, it really hit home. I understood Coach Cray. I just had no idea how to prove to her that I was happy to play on her team.

I was the best goalie on the team. But it wasn't going to be enough. I hadn't told my dad yet that I'd started off on the wrong foot, and I was going to do my best to make sure he never found out. If he got involved, I'd lose all chance at earning Coach's respect. And I was determined to. I hadn't gotten this good by backing down.

Classes were kicking my ass as well. I'd heard that college could be tougher than high school, but I'd been so focused on hockey that I'd ignored thinking about classes. Another mistake. I planned to major in business, and for some reason, I'd thought it would be a good idea to get rid of all the non-business classes first, before I hopefully became a starter and had to focus more on hockey. That meant I had a bunch of classes that didn't interest me much, and the profs were piling on the course work.

Hockey wasn't my happy place the way it always had been. Penny was spending a lot of time with her cross-country guy, so I felt like a third wheel in my own room. I figured it had to get better, but then Coach dropped the bomb about how we were doing the preseason exhibition game this year, and suddenly, things hadn't been that bad in comparison.

4

Sebastien

My run didn't give me any magic solutions, but I managed to get my brain mostly in gear. By that, I mean that I was able to focus on hockey and was left tired enough that the rest couldn't mess me up too much.

Last year, I'd hardly noticed the women's team. Since we shared the rink, we weren't there at the same time very often. We did sometimes use the workout rooms together. Not the scheduled times, but if we went in for extra workouts.

This year, I couldn't help but notice. It came as no surprise that Faith worked out a lot. As much as I'd like to forget she was around, I couldn't. I only saw her at a distance, and I never saw her looking at me. She was never near a place I was working out, and my brain was stupid enough that I had to remind it that was good. Other than that, the first week or so went by pretty well. I met up with Holly for meals and studying, but hockey was my first priority. She was supportive and let me do what I needed to do without feeling guilty. As long as I texted her so she knew I wasn't ghosting her, she was good. I was a lucky guy.

Then, a week in, Coach dropped a bombshell.

Last year, we'd played an exhibition game against the

women's team as part of the pre-season. Ticket sales had gone to a charity, and it had given the women some exposure. When Coach mentioned an exhibition game, I realized that playing against the women this year would be different if Faith was in net.

I heard one of the freshmen ask his buddy if they'd be facing that goalie on the women's team again. I knew he meant Faith. We would not be able to ignore her. *I* would not be able to ignore her. Would I?

Fortunately, I spent the least amount of time in the offensive zone near the other team's goalie. It's not like I wouldn't have to face Faith in net, assuming she played, which she would, but not that often. I could ignore her for a few shifts, right? Of course, it wasn't going to be that easy.

"We're doing something new this year," Coach said. "We're going to mix up the teams."

I wasn't the only one confused. Cooper frowned over at me. We'd been paired up in practices and were pretty sure we'd be playing together a lot this year. What did Coach mean by mixing up the teams? Did that mean splitting us up? Playing us as forwards? Or, hellacious thought, goalies?

He could tell we weren't following, and his grin was evil. "We're going to have co-ed teams for the exhibition game."

A groan went through the locker room. I wasn't a math major, but I knew that meant there was a fifty per cent chance I could be on the same team as Faith. Instead of playing on the opposite end of the ice, I might be playing in front of her. We couldn't ignore each other on the same team.

Fuck.

"Teams are posted. Anyone in this locker room on the losing team gets suicides."

It was supposed to be a friendly game, but Coach was making sure we were going to play and not loaf on the ice. And since we'd probably be split up fifty-fifty, half the guys in the locker room would be on the losing team. Then I realized he was going to be coaching one team while Coach Cray, the women's coach would be coaching the other team. I wasn't sure which would be worse, being on Coach's team and losing, or being on the other team and winning. I hoped he would win. And that I would be on his team.

"There's a practice for the co-ed teams on Saturday morning before the game Saturday night."

He left the room, and conversation buzzed. Some of the guys were upset they had to play with women. Some of the guys thought it was great.

Cooper leaned over. "Which do you want, to play for Coach or against him?"

I shook my head. "No idea. The coaches are going to take this seriously."

"I wonder if they drafted the teams or picked players randomly?"

I considered that. "Coach would never go for random."

"So his team will have the best of our team, and the worst of the women's team." That was simplistic but probably close to the truth.

"Let's find out where we are."

The team listings had been emailed out to us. Cooper had his phone out first, so we opened up the attachment and looked for our names.

The players were listed by position, so we started with Coach's team. I was surprised to see Coop and I were both there. We were the second defensive pairing, but if Coach wanted us... I looked up at the forwards. Yeah, he had his top line there. His top defensive line was with Coach Cray. Coach Keller was going to lean on offense. Coach Cray was going to have the stronger defense, so she'd want to have Faith on her team. Tension I hadn't been aware of leeched out of my shoulders.

Not great, but the better of two options.

Faith was a secret weapon. I'd heard from Cooper how well she'd done at that first rookie practice, but Coach Keller hadn't been on the ice then, so our coach didn't know how good she was.

It wasn't like he was going to study up the stats on players who weren't his to draft for an exhibition game team. I wasn't prepared when I looked at the goalies for our team and saw Faith's name.

That was good for our chances, but that meant Faith and I were playing together. Both on defense. That was going to screw with the mutual ignoring strategy we'd been following.

Fuck. Me.

Faith

I'd been doing such an excellent job of pretending Seb didn't exist. Now, we were going to play on a team together. We'd had an unspoken agreement to pretend we didn't know each other. At least, I thought that was what we were doing. The few times we'd seen each other in the workout room, Seb hadn't come to say hi.

Not sure what I'd have done if he had. A year ago, a heavy weight to the groin wouldn't have been outside the realm of possibilities. Actually, I'd pictured that a few times. Fondly. Now I didn't know. I wasn't going to hurt him. I hoped I could treat him like any other teammate. Any other cheating scumbag… Okay, I wasn't completely over what he'd done.

Still, big picture, he'd done me a favor. I wouldn't forget the lesson. Avoid athletes, at least when it came to dating. There were athletes who could be faithful, and there were cheaters who didn't play sports. Obviously. It's just that the odds were better that the athlete would be faced with more temptation and be told that it was okay to mess around. Boys would just be boys.

I wasn't surprised that Coach Cray didn't keep me on her team. She hadn't said they'd drafted the teams instead of drawing names out of a hat, but it was obvious. Our top offensive forwards were all on Coach Cray's team, and so were the second defensive pairings.

I got the message. I could play with the men.

It didn't change how I was going to play. Whether I was playing for Coach Cray or the guys' coach, I was going to bring my A game. Eventually, she'd have to accept that I was good. Wouldn't she?

I was one of the first players on the ice for the co-ed practice. There were too many players for us all to be on the ice at the same time, so Coach Keller and his patched-up team had the first slot. I was calling that a lost coin toss.

The women were standing together, and so were the guys. Separate groups. I was on my own. As goalie, I had my own warmup, and I was the only female goalie on this team. I was stretching by myself when the two men's goalies came over and joined me. We were the oddballs on the team anyway since we warmed up differently. I appreciated them reaching out. They'd heard about the freshman shoot-out. We talked a bit about that. They were interested in where I'd played, and I asked what I should know about the skaters we'd be facing. They didn't ask about the women, and I noted that. They didn't seem to be too worried about the women who'd be taking shots on them. I'd already had shooting drills with the women in practice, and these guys were in for a surprise.

Coach blew his whistle, and we skated in to hear what he had to say.

With the game tonight, this practice was mostly a chance for the team to figure out how to play together. No one wanted to leave all their best stuff on the ice before the game. Each goalie would play one period during the game, and the three of us would take turns in the two nets during the practice.

Seb was there, and so was Cooper. They were teamed up on defense. Coach Keller put me in net from the beginning. He wanted to know what I could do. I showed him. I knew Zoe and Rocky, the women's defense pair on this exhibition team, and we'd worked well together in practices. There was no problem communicating with them, and they picked up any rebounds I sent them quickly. Coach Keller appeared to approve of us.

Then I was playing with Seb and Cooper. I had to be more alert. I wasn't sure how we'd work together. Ignoring Seb was not a possibility, not when we were teammates. I knew Seb would be the guy to hang back when play headed to the other end of the ice. I'd watched him play for years, knew his game almost as well as he did himself. Still, he was slow to join in the first rush our practice team got, which meant he didn't want to leave me back here alone. That indicated to everyone on the ice that he didn't think I could cover on my own.

Oh, hell no.

"Move your fucking ass, Seb!"

I hadn't thought, just yelled it out by habit. I didn't need him to babysit me back here. My girls knew I could take care of myself, and I could already see the problems snowballing from these guys not trusting their female teammates. Seb skated ahead and had just gotten into the offensive zone when a missed pass brought everyone back down to me. Fortunately, Cooper had legs and got to the puck soon after it crossed the blue line. He shot it back down ice, and Coach blew the whistle.

Everyone piled back into our zone for a faceoff. Seb was in front of me, waiting for the puck drop, but Coach was talking to a couple of forwards. I didn't think again, just spoke the words that were waiting on my tongue. "What the fuck, Seb? I don't need a babysitter. Do your job."

I didn't need him hovering over me like a granny, giving Coach Keller the idea I couldn't handle myself. I was a freshman. I had a lot to prove. Seb might be a cheating scumbag, but he didn't need to make this game tougher for me. Seb didn't look at me, but I saw him shrug. *Fine, just play your damn game, Hunter.*

At the next break in play, Cooper skated by and tapped my pads. "Guess we should have known after the freshman practice that you can take care of yourself."

"Hell yes."

"And you aren't going to clutch your pearls if we swear." He smirked.

I shoved up my face guard. "That was nothing. If someone gets in my crease, I'll really get upset. And loud."

Cooper narrowed his eyes. I wondered if he was one of those guys who didn't like women who swore. He'd seemed cool at the party a couple of weeks ago, but assholes sometimes had good fronts.

"You're from Canada, right?"

I nodded. Canadians might be known to be polite, but hockey players weren't going to say sorry all the time.

"Toronto?"

"Yeah. Why?"

"Just working out something."

I had no idea what. The coach blew his whistle, and play started back up, so I put down my visor and got back into the playing zone.

Sebastien

I admit, I freaked out a bit playing with Faith. I couldn't get out of my head. I was slow to join play in the offensive zone and spent too much time watching the net when we were in our own zone. Cooper noticed. Of course, he did. Fortunately, Briggs got moved into net after a bit, and I could focus on my own fucking game for the rest of practice.

Coach told me to get my head out of my ass, which was deserved, and I promised to do better. He gave me a sharp look but let it go. A lot of the guys had had problems playing with the women. The women didn't appear to have any trouble. The guys were tentative about checking and gave them too much space. That lasted about ten minutes, until they handed us our asses and Coach blew up at us. Then we smartened up. I still missed a couple of checks, but this was an exhibition game, so we didn't need to play that hard. Except, of course, we wanted to avoid suicide drills.

After practise, we went back to the hockey house to grab some food and rest. This was the first pre-season game, so we were following game-day schedule.

I went up to my room, and Coop knocked on the doorframe.

I looked up from my textbook. I wanted to get on top of my reading. I'd told Holly I'd be tied up until after the game. The women's team was hosting a party after, and I'd promised her we'd go together. Faith was not going to mess with my head anymore.

"Got a minute, Hunter?"

I put my book down. I was on my bed, and he sat on the desk chair.

"What's up?"

He stared at me for a minute, and I wondered what was wrong.

"Is Faith the one?"

I froze. I couldn't speak. I wasn't ready to talk about Faith. How the hell had he worked this out?

"Devereaux. You two obviously know each other, but you pretend you don't." I shook my head a bit, and he held up a hand. "She didn't swear at any of us or call us by our first names."

At least Faith was the one who'd messed up.

"Plus, you knew she'd done that newbie shoot-out thing before, but then you disappeared. And her name is Faith."

I'd mentioned her name last year when it had all gone down. I hadn't said she was a hockey player. I hadn't said much about her to anyone those first couple of weeks before the big blowup, but I had said her name. I'd hoped no one had remembered.

"She's from Toronto, and you were playing like someone else while she was in net today."

Cooper was listing everything off like I was on the stand and he was cross-examining me. Had he switched to a prelaw major? He leaned back, waiting for me to respond. He knew. No way I could deny it. I forced my muscles to relax. I hadn't committed a crime. It was just embarrassing.

"Yeah, she's the ex."

I'd gone out with a couple of girls last year before Holly, but Faith was *the* ex. The others hadn't been a big deal. With those girls, we'd gone out and had some fun, but it had never been like with Faith.

"Have you talked to her?"

I'd said her name and almost kissed her back on that first day, but no, we hadn't talked.

"Only when she called me out on the ice today."

"That means she doesn't know what really happened?"

I shook my head.

I'd been so drunk when I talked to her last year that I still didn't know exactly what I'd told her. I shouldn't have tried to contact her until I was sober. My teammates had tried to convince me. They'd taken my phone. I'd been petrified she'd find out from someone before I could explain, so I'd found a phone and called her. Whatever I'd told her hadn't explained it clearly. I'd made it sound like something had happened.

That misunderstanding had been too much for her. She'd never taken another call from me and blocked me on every avenue I could think of to reach out to her. I'd been desperate enough to try a lot. If the team hadn't stopped me, I'd have driven to Toronto, if I could have found a car.

It had been hard to accept that we were over. It had hurt that she hadn't thought we were worth enough to at least let me explain. I'd thought we were going to be forever. I'd been wrong. And hell if I wanted to talk about it now, not with Cooper *or* Faith.

"You should tell her. Let her know what really happened."

Like she would listen to anything I said. "Why? I've moved on, and I'm with Holly now." I almost flinched. I was with Holly, but it wasn't like Faith and I had been. To be fair, Holly and I hadn't been together that long yet. I'd been with Faith for most of two years. Of course, the thing with Faith had been more intense. It had ripped me to shreds when she'd cut things off, so I was okay with things being a little lighter right now.

"Sure about that?"

"What the hell are you talking about? Of course, I'm with Holly." I wasn't going to admit I'd just been comparing my feelings for Holly and Faith.

"I mean," He was speaking slowly, like he thought I was stupid. "Have you really moved on from Faith?"

Fucker. Maybe I hadn't totally, but I was working on it. "Why wouldn't I have moved on? It's been a year."

"Maybe because she still doesn't know what really happened, and you two can't even look at each other?"

"Not your business, Coop."

He shrugged. "You're good now, you know you didn't cheat, and you've got another girlfriend. But what about Faith?"

I frowned. "What about her? I don't know if she's got a boyfriend, if that's what you mean."

He shook his head. "She thinks you cheated on her."

I rolled my eyes. "Yes, I'm quite aware of that."

"How do you think she feels about that?"

"She refused to talk to me, so I'm guessing she isn't too thrilled."

He looked at the ceiling. "Can you look at it from her side for a minute? She believes that the first chance that rolled around, you either forgot about her or decided she wasn't worth it and cheated on her. Fucked someone else. Decided she wasn't enough."

The words hit hard. I'd felt this way once when I hit the boards helmet first. Like I was suddenly drifting above my body, not really attached to it anymore. Shit. I hadn't thought about that part of it. Faith had been so perfect for me that it was hard to think she might have felt she wasn't good enough. How had I missed that? Because I'd been so hurt myself, I'd felt like *I* wasn't good enough. Had she felt that way, too?

Damn Coop. What was I supposed to do with that now? How could I explain what had really happened without sounding like I was just trying to get her back? Especially after that run-in at the arena, the one where I'd almost kissed her. Plus, there was Holly.

It wasn't fair to her, and Faith would think I was two-timing Holly. Why the hell did Coop have to bring this up now?

"She won't talk to me. It's just going to upset her if I try to bring it up. It's better to let it go."

"Sure about that?"

"Yeah, I'm sure. It's ancient history now."

"I hope you can play tonight when she's in net."

"Don't worry about me."

Cooper stood up. "Okay. I just don't want to do suicides because you're wound up about our goalie."

I gave him the finger. He left, and I tried to settle back to my reading. Damn him. I'd been doing fine. Now I couldn't concentrate. Should I try to talk to Faith? I mean, not to try to get back together with her. A year had passed. I was with Holly now. For all I knew, Faith had a boyfriend. That thought settled on me. She probably did. Why not?

There was no reason that should bother me. I should be glad for her. I was. Really.

I had no idea what the guy would be like, but I knew one thing. It wouldn't be a hockey player.

5

Sebastien

The arena was full. Hockey was popular here, and this game was for a good cause. Cooper and I were starting for Coach Keller's team, and Faith was not the starter.

She was playing the second period.

That helped. Once the game started, I could concentrate on playing. It was new playing with other people, let alone women. I hadn't ever done that. Last year, we'd played against the women's team. They'd been good in practice, and they were even better in a game situation. By the time we were five minutes in, we weren't thinking that some of the players were a different gender. They were players, and we started to play as hard against them as they were playing against us.

We ended the first period tied, one all. Cooper and I were usually on the ice playing against the men's top line, and we knew how those guys worked. We didn't know the women as well, but the coaches would put out the women's defense against the women. The crowd didn't like that as much.

In the second period, Coach started Faith. And when Coach Cray put out a starting line that included two of her women and one of our guys, Coach Keller countered with me and one of the women defense players. Things got a lot more interesting.

The crowd roared whenever the women won a faceoff against the men, or whenever the men stole a puck from the women. I managed to play the way I was supposed to even with Faith around. In fact, we played well together. I found it easy to pick out her voice when she called out comments and warnings. She bounced rebounds my way like she always knew where I'd be on the ice. We used to practice together, and somehow, we'd gotten past the awkwardness and that familiarity had returned. On the ice, at least.

Our team managed a goal that period, but nothing got by Faith. We didn't give the other team a lot of chances, but there was a breakdown in communication on one play that had Coach cursing. I was glad I was on the bench, because he was pissed. The other team came at Faith two on one, but she handled it beautifully. And that was against their top scorers. It shouldn't have mattered to me. After all, we weren't together. We weren't even friends. But I was proud of her.

Cooper tapped her pads at the end of the period since she was done for the game after that. I thought of doing it, but she moved away before I had a chance, and I had no idea if that was on purpose or not. I didn't know which option I preferred.

Faith

I was dreading and looking forward to this party. I'd played well and was ready to celebrate our win, but I knew my time of avoiding Seb was winding down fast.

This time, Penny wasn't going with me. She had a date with her cross-country guy, but she kept her promise and helped me get ready. Again, she moaned over my wardrobe. The skirt was brought back out, and she lent me some jewelry and helped with my makeup. I'd gone and bought some, partly to make her happy, partly to give myself some confidence for this kind of thing.

The party was at the women's hockey house. I knew my teammates now, not as well as I'd like, but I wasn't going into strange territory. We'd had a couple of team get-togethers at the house, so at least it was ground I knew. Maybe next year I'd be living there. This year they were full, and the school liked freshmen in the dorms. Except somehow the men's hockey players were exempt from that.

Maybe Seb wouldn't be there. He hadn't been at the last one. I thought my chances of missing him were good.

They weren't.

I ran into a couple of teammates climbing the steps, so at least I didn't arrive on my own. They congratulated me on my scoreless period. I did the same on a goal they'd paired up on. We entered the house together and paused in the doorway while we got our bearings. Our eardrums were overwhelmed by the volume of the music.

The first person I saw was Seb.

My stomach did a weird little roll, seeing him there, wearing a nice shirt with his jeans. I wondered if he'd see me. If he'd think I looked good, too.

Then I caught movement and saw the petite brunette with her arm wrapped around his waist. He had his arm around her as well.

My stomach wasn't roiling anymore. It flattened like a pancake.

My teammates moved to the kitchen where the drinks were, and I kept tight with them as we moved through the rooms. I carefully didn't look anywhere near Seb again.

I took a solo cup, cheered with my teammates as we chatted about the game, and in the back of my mind, *he's got a girlfriend* played on repeat. I shouldn't care. I didn't want him, not after what he'd done. I hadn't been waiting for him, and I hadn't come here to see him again.

Yes, he had a girlfriend, and I didn't want a boyfriend. I'd had offers. Well, one serious one. But right now, I was going to focus only on hockey and enough on school that I could play hockey. I'd been a mess after Seb called that night a year ago, and it had affected my game. I wasn't going to risk that again. And when I wanted to find someone, when I wanted companionship, I wouldn't be looking at anyone on the hockey team.

Fool me once…

I was distracted, so when someone right behind me spoke with a masculine voice, I jumped. My face started to flush, until I realized it wasn't Seb. Right. Why would it be? I turned to find Cooper standing behind me, smirking as if he had some idea what I was thinking. Nope. Not unless Seb had been talking, but even then…

Mental slap. Not going to think about Seb again.

There were calls of "Cooper" from people in the room. I raised my cup and said "Blondie!"

He reached out and tugged on a strand of my hair. "Good job today, Blondie."

I slapped his hand away.

"Call me Dev so that people don't get confused. You know, about which Blondie should answer?"

"Yeah, but I'm a junior, so I have seniority. You can call me Coop, and I'll call you Blondie."

"I'd sooner do an hour of crunches."

Coop touched his cup to mine. "I'll see what I can arrange."

He really didn't need to arrange anything. Coach Cray was out for my blood already.

Cooper leaned close to my ear. "Let's go somewhere quieter."

I snorted. "Is this your move, Blondie?"

"Do you want it to be, Blondie?" he asked.

"I don't live here, Coop, so I couldn't take you up to my room even if I wanted to. Why don't you find someone who does?"

He cocked his head, never losing that smug, confident smile.

"If I make a move, you'll know it. I just want to talk to you about something."

I was curious. I had no idea what this guy would want to talk about. We'd had fun talking hockey at the last party, but that didn't require quiet or privacy.

He started moving through the crowd, heading to the patio doors off the back of the kitchen. Obviously, he knew his way around here. Not really a surprise. I surprised myself a bit by following. He slid open the door, and we were on the deck. A few others were out here, stealing a clandestine cigarette or joint. He kept walking, waving as a few people called his name, until we were in a corner at the back of the fence. It wasn't totally private, but it was quiet, and no one was paying attention to us.

It was cool, but not unpleasantly so. Despite the short skirt, I was warm enough. I tended to run warm. Penny and I couldn't agree on a room temp that worked for both of us.

Cooper didn't say anything at first, so I looked up at the stars. Even though I was from Canada, this place was farther north than Toronto. I was from the big city, with a population of millions, and Burlington was a fraction of that. The air was different, and the stars were more visible.

It was nice.

"You're Seb's Faith, aren't you?"

My head whipped around to meet his gaze. I felt my mouth drop open, but I had no words to say. It was just…unexpected and right and wrong all at the same time. Then anger kicked in. What the hell had Seb been saying?

"I'm not Seb's anything." I spoke each word clearly, leaving no room for doubt.

Cooper didn't speak, and I turned to leave. I didn't know what he and Seb were up to, but I wanted no part of it. This wasn't something I was willing to talk about, ever.

"Sorry, Faith. That was the wrong way to say it. Let me try again. Were you dating Seb when he arrived here as a freshman?"

I turned back and crossed my arms. I'd still like to walk away, but it might be good to know what Seb had said, what people around here thought about me based on his words. I was already in trouble with my coach. If there was more, more I had to deal with, it was better to know it.

"What did he say?"

Cooper leaned back. He could relax. This had fuck all to do with him.

"I guess that's a yes. He didn't say much. He told us he had a girlfriend back home, so he wasn't interested in girls at that first party we had. He said his girlfriend couldn't make it that weekend, so he'd just drink a bit, since he was lonely."

I snorted. I didn't know what he'd told his teammates, and I really didn't care. Actions reveal the person inside. Words are just the coverup people use to impress others.

"He did get pretty drunk. He said he'd been hardcore training all summer and hadn't been drinking. I was a little embarrassed for him. The beer we have at parties isn't that strong."

"I don't care."

It didn't excuse him. If he was sober enough to have sex, he was sober enough to know what he was doing. That he was fucking someone else.

"His room was up on the third floor last year, so I helped him get up there. Guy couldn't judge where the steps were. I thought he was gone for the night."

I wanted to leave. I didn't need to hear the details about my boyfriend cheating. But part of me was fascinated. Something screwed up inside me made me want to know what had happened. I wasn't surprised the long-distance thing hadn't worked. I'd told him it wouldn't. I just hadn't thought he'd cheat before the first month was out.

"We didn't hear him yelling until a couple of hours later."

I made myself stay still, unmoving. Cooper was relaxed, leaning against the fence, but I saw how he was watching me. He wanted to see my response. He was one sick bastard. Like I wanted to know what Seb had been doing during sex? Cheating sex?

I wasn't going to blink first. Now it was a competition. Would I break before he finished his story? I put up my mental blockers, the ones that had gotten me through those first weeks after I'd cut off all contact with Seb. This fucker was not going to see me flinch.

"We done?"

"I got to his room first, since I was in mine on the second floor. I thought he'd had a nightmare. I remember thinking I hope he doesn't scream like that all the time, because that would get old fast.

"Guy looked terrified, and I couldn't figure out why. There was a hot chick in bed with him, and we could see they'd been making out. Her top was off, but she still had on the rest of her clothes."

Like I really needed that visual in my memory bank.

"She was freaked out, too. Seb started babbling about Faith, and it was supposed to be Faith, and why did the girl ask for a condom. He was pretty much in tears.

"I picked up her top, passed it to her, and she put in on. I asked her what the fuck had happened. Seb wasn't making any sense, and she seemed fine. She said she'd gone upstairs, found Seb sleeping there, and slid in beside him. She was obviously a puck bunny hoping to nail one of the freshmen. She said it had been going great, but then she'd asked him if he had a condom, and he'd freaked and started shouting."

Cooper was watching me closely, and I was doing my best to not show any expression.

"I passed her off to someone and tried to figure out what the hell Seb's problem was. I've never found a hot chick in bed wanting to fuck something to scream about."

My mind was racing now. I was trying to remember what Seb had said on that call, and how it lined up with this story Cooper was spinning, and why he'd be covering for Seb. Was Seb afraid

I'd tell the story around campus and women wouldn't want to date him? As if. I'd already seen how the hockey team was treated here. The men's team. A bit of infidelity wouldn't stop some people.

"Seb said cheating was a total deal-breaker for his girlfriend, and he had to call her to explain." Cooper came to stand in front of me. "We could all see that was a bad idea. I didn't know why he was so determined to call and confess he'd made out with a chick. He said he'd thought it was her, the girlfriend. That she'd changed her mind and come to stay with him. And something about grandmothers and condoms, and that he had to tell her before anyone else did.

"He wasn't making any sense, and we convinced him to wait until he was sober to call. I took his phone because I didn't trust him. I thought we'd sober him up in the morning, talk it through, and persuade him not to say anything to you."

He paused in his story, and I forgot Cooper was standing in front of me. I was revisiting the past, trying to take these two contradictory realities and see if they could coexist. Cooper's story was that Seb had gone to bed drunk, made out with a girl in his bed who he'd thought was me. I got the part about the condom and the grandmother. I had planned to visit campus that weekend. We'd been looking forward to spending a whole weekend together. But my grandmother had a stroke, so I'd cancelled.

Seb had been my first, and I'd been his. We'd gone from friends, to kissing, to working around all the bases. When we'd decided to sleep together, I'd made sure I did everything right. I'd started taking the pill, and we'd bought condoms. Putting that condom on for the first time had been awkward, but we'd laughed together. Then, well, we hadn't been laughing. We'd both become fans of sex. We were young and horny and got together every chance we had.

I'd had a reaction to latex condoms. I got itchy, scabby skin in a part of the body nobody wants to have itchy and scabby. We'd done some online research and found out about latex allergies. We'd decided we could trust each other for STD's since we'd both been virgins, and I was on the pill to take care of a pregnancy. I'd been too embarrassed to talk to my doctor back then about my irritated girl parts.

Now I knew more about it and had non-latex condoms. But yeah, that part of Cooper's story made sense. If Seb had thought it was me with him, asking about a condom would have been a wakeup call that it wasn't.

I tried to remember his exact words, but I couldn't. I'd heard sorry, girl, bed, and condom. That was a cheating narrative. Except maybe it wasn't. And I didn't know how to feel. There was a little zing of what might be hope, and a heavy zap of grief for what I might have missed. And through it all was a lot of suspicion.

I needed time to work this through. First, I had to figure out if anything Cooper was telling me was true. Then I had to figure out what it meant if he wasn't lying. It was like the ice had shifted beneath my feet, and I wasn't sure of my footing anymore.

Could it be the truth? In either case, I had questions.

"Why are you telling me this?"

It didn't change things. Seb and I weren't together. He had a girlfriend. Had he asked Cooper to tell me this story to see if he could get back with me? Was he going to cheat on this new girl, too? Had he cheated on me? He might not have. It was hard to change that fact in my memory banks.

"I told Seb to tell you, but he didn't think you'd listen to him, or you'd think he was trying to hook up with you again."

Cooper had a couple of inches on Seb, so I had to look a little higher up to meet his gaze.

"You told me anyway."

"I thought you needed to hear it."

"Why?"

I couldn't imagine why Seb's teammate had decided to tell me this story if Seb wasn't behind it. I couldn't accept it as truth without knowing there was a valid reason for Cooper to tell me.

"Because if someone cheats on you, it messes with your head. You wonder what you did, or what was wrong with you."

He had a point. But— "If someone cheats, that's on them. I blame the cheater, not the person who gets cheated on," I said.

He tapped my temple. "That's the thing. You can tell yourself that, but inside, you still wonder." Cooper stepped back into the shadows where I couldn't see his face.

He was right. I could tell myself all day long that it wasn't my fault Seb had cheated, but those stupid questions kept coming back. *What if I'd been there that weekend? What if I'd called him from the hospital, or after we got home?*

I tried to cut them off, especially when they got to *What if I was more feminine? What if I was shorter, thinner, prettier?"*

I knew they were bad questions. But I'd been taller, bigger, less-girlie girl all my life. There'd been comments. I'd tried to shrug them off, but some had stuck. If Cooper's story was true, it didn't mean Seb and I would get back together. But if he didn't cheat, it meant there was nothing wrong with me. Or with Seb. I hadn't somehow trusted a cheater. It meant maybe my judgement wasn't total shit. Cooper was right. Knowing that Seb hadn't cheated would change things for me. I appreciated it, but I wasn't going to let him know how much. Not until I knew the truth, and still not then, probably. A guy like this didn't need any positive reinforcement.

"You have a point there, Blondie."

"Of course, I do."

"This doesn't mean I want to get back with Seb. I know he's got a girlfriend."

"Yeah, he's weird that way."

My first response to seeing Seb with the tiny brunette hadn't been to be besties with her, but I hadn't thought it weird. "Weird?"

"When we finally got him to move on, we wanted him to have

some fun. But he ended up dating his rebound girl for two months. The guy should be enjoying his single life, but he's all about relationships."

I wondered about that comment. I was sure Cooper had a story he wasn't sharing. That wasn't fair, not when he knew all about mine. "You're not a relationship guy?"

I saw his teeth in the darkness. "Nah. You can't cheat on someone if you're single, right? You should approve."

I'd heard too many similar lines from guys my dad repre-sented. I didn't have to be on board with this kind of twisted logic. "I'd like to think there's an option between cheating and single. Like dating and not cheating."

"We all have our dreams, Blondie. Relationships are not one of mine. Now, if you needed a rebound…"

He probably couldn't see me rolling my eyes in the dark, but this was just so typical. "How self-sacrificing of you. But don't worry. I've already rebounded. I haven't been pining this last year."

"You mind going away, Coop?" a new voice suddenly spoke behind me. "Faith and I need to talk."

6

Sebastien

Part of me wanted to avoid the party. I didn't want to be around Faith with Cooper watching my every move. I didn't need him judging how well I'd moved on. And then there was Holly. Cooper would be watching me with her as well. But I'd promised Holly, and she wanted to go. Our parties were good, and people liked to be there. So I was there. With Holly. And totally on edge. I kept one eye out for Faith and one on Cooper. It was making me cross-eyed and giving me a headache.

I'd missed Faith arriving, but I did spot her after she came in. I saw her go to the kitchen with some of her teammates. I knew that tall figure, the way she moved, the blond hair. But wait... It wasn't back in a braid?

I stared. I mean, I'd been with the girl for two years, and she'd never worn skirts or dresses. I'd tried to convince her she was beautiful, which she was, but I'd never gotten through to her. I hadn't cared what she wore, but I'd wished she'd felt comfortable wearing whatever the hell she wanted. She looked good, more than good. She worked hard to be that fit, and I'd found it a total turn on.

Tonight, she'd finally embraced her looks. A skirt, makeup,

and her hair down. I'd never seen her hair down, except when we'd been...

A twitch from my dick told me it was a bad idea to revisit those particular memories here at a party with another girl. Maybe Faith had had reason to not trust me.

I shook my head and pulled my gaze away. I looked for Cooper and found him heading toward Faith. *Fuck.* Who knew what he'd say to her? Next thing, he had a hand on her back. I wanted to push between the two of them and keep him away from her. But I couldn't. I had no right. I was supposed to be enjoying this party with my girlfriend.

The two of them headed outside. What the actual fuck was he doing? Trying to put a move on her? Tell her shit that was none of his business? I started moving but felt a tug on my arm. Holly was frowning at me.

Fuck. Fuck, fuck, fuck.

Great time to figure out Cooper was right. I wasn't over Faith. I did need to talk to her, clear the air so I could move on. Not with her. Faith and I were over. I got that. Holly deserved my attention, and I wasn't going to show Faith she was right about me by dumping Holly for another chance to date Faith.

Where the hell had that thought come from? I wasn't that kind of asshole. Holly and I were together, and I'd do what I needed to work things out with her.

There was nothing to work out. We were good. It was just these memories messing me up. I needed to get this settled, and then my life could go back to normal. Really settled this time.

"Seb, what's the problem?" Holly was frowning and rubbing her hand up and down my back, trying to sooth me because I was tensed up. Who knew what my face looked like?

I jerked a hand through my hair. "I, uh..." I had no idea what to say.

Holly tugged me away from the kitchen, away from where Coop and Faith had gone. She pulled me into a corner and crossed her arms.

"Who's that girl?"

I wanted to ask what girl, but I didn't need to act stupid. Who knew how long I'd been staring at Faith? I closed my eyes, gathered some air and courage, and opened my eyes again to answer. "That's Faith."

Her brow creased. "Faith? The girl from Canada? The one who broke up with you last year when she thought you cheated?"

I nodded.

Holly's gaze moved back to the kitchen, but Faith and Cooper were missing.

"Why is she here?"

Holly did not sound happy. Damn it. I should have told her. I'd made it a big deal by not telling her. How did I explain this?

"She's on the women's team. The hockey team."

Holly went still. I could almost read the thoughts going through her head. We'd played with the women's team today, and Holly had watched the game. There was no way I could pretend I hadn't known Faith was here.

"Why didn't you tell me?"

Yep, there was the million-dollar question.

"I thought it would upset you. I didn't want to do that."

Her lips thinned. Yeah, that hadn't worked.

"I'm sorry, that was stupid of me."

"Have you talked to her?"

I shook my head. "Nothing except hockey stuff when we were on the ice."

"Do you want to?"

Did I? Part of me did. Another part of me wanted to escape this house and run. I might not ever come to a party again.

"I don't know. I wasn't going to, but maybe I should." I remembered what Cooper had said about how believing I'd cheated on her might have hurt Faith.

Holly bit her lip. "Seb, I know you didn't cheat. You told me that. But I know it's different for guys like you."

"What?" I had no idea what she was talking about.

"You play hockey. There's a reason there are more girls at these parties than guys. They want to brag about being with a hockey player. And if you played professionally, there would be even more women who would want to sleep with you, right?"

"Yes, but—"

"I'm just saying I understand that. I'm not like her, your ex. I know you'll be under pressure, and I'm not going to freak out. You can be honest with me, and I'm not going to cut you off that way. We can always talk and work things out."

I stared at Holly, trying to make sense of what she was saying.

Did she not believe me when I said I hadn't cheated? Or was she saying she didn't care? I felt a little dizzy, like I'd had too much cheap beer. I took a look at my cup, half full. Was there something in it?

"You wouldn't care if I cheated on you?" My voice sounded off to me, but this whole conversation was off.

"Obviously, I'd care, Sebastien. I'm just saying that your case is a little different than regular guys, and we'd work with that."

Right. My case was different. I played hockey. Ice slithered down my spine.

This was exactly the shit that made Faith the way she was. Her dad thought his case was different because he used to play hockey, and his clients, the ones who got in trouble when they were caught with hookers or sports groupies, they thought they were special because of the sports they played.

I hated that. I hated that some people thought they had permission to hurt others because of their job, or fame, or wealth. I didn't understand someone like Holly who was willing to accept that. Did she really believe she didn't deserve the same kind of commitment from me because I play a sport?

Or did she think it was an option for her, too? I looked at her like I was seeing her for the first time. Like she was a stranger. She didn't know me, not if she thought I'd be like that. Maybe she didn't need to know me. Maybe she just needed to know I wore a jersey, that she was a hockey player's girlfriend.

I didn't feel dizzy anymore. I was hot with embarrassment and anger. I didn't want to be with someone who saw only me as a hockey player. For so much of my life, the only value people had found in me had been in my ability to play hockey. They didn't care about who else I was.

I'd hoped someday I'd find someone who was interested in the guy under the jersey. I'd had that with Faith. The last thing she'd wanted was to be with a hockey player, so I knew she had seen me, the real me, not the player. She'd wanted me in spite of me being a hockey player. That's what I wanted in a relationship. But it seemed it wasn't what I had with Holly.

I did need to talk to Faith. But I also needed to talk to my girlfriend.

Not here, not at a party. Because to break up with Holly in the middle of a party would be an asshole move, and I didn't want to be an asshole. But neither could I stand here and pretend what she'd said hadn't affected me.

"I'm going to get a drink." I turned, headed for the kitchen, and went on out through the doors.

Things were blowing up with my girlfriend. I wanted to know if the same thing was happening with my teammate and my ex.

I wasn't thrilled to see Coop still talking to Faith. Even less thrilled when he volunteered to be her rebound. My hands had curled into fists before I'd realized what I was doing. But she didn't take him up on it, not Faith. Instead, she told him she'd already rebounded.

Of course, she had. She believed I'd cheated.

I had no right to be upset. I'd rebounded, too, but I still hated the thought of Faith with someone else. Which was another kind of asshole behavior, but apparently, I had more of that in me than I liked.

I moved closer, and Coop looked over at me.

"You mind going away, Coop? Faith and I need to talk."

I couldn't read Coop's face in the dark, but he moved aside.

"Play nice, kids."

Then it was just Faith and me.

She turned to face me, but I couldn't read her expression in the dark, either. I didn't know what Coop had been up to. I had a good idea what it was though.

"What did Cooper tell you?"

I suspected he'd decided Faith needed to hear the truth. He was probably right, but I should have been the one to tell her. Except she wouldn't have listened.

"He gave me a story about what happened last year."

I knew it. But Faith was obviously still skeptical. "What did he say?"

I mean, I knew he would have told the truth. He knew most of it. But I wanted to hear how Faith felt about it, and I thought if she told me what he'd said in her words, I'd know what was up with her.

Faith crossed her arms. "He said enough that I'm here willing to listen to you."

He'd told her. But she wanted to hear it from me. Maybe to see if the stories matched. I didn't care. This was my chance to clear the air, to get closure, whatever. I was taking it.

"I didn't sleep with the girl, the one who was in my bed that night, but I thought it was you, so we made out."

I had cheated that much, but not knowingly.

"How could you think it was me?"

My knee was jiggling again. "I drank too much at the party. I felt sorry for myself. I know, your grandmother was sick, but I'd really needed to see you. I went up to bed, and I dunno, passed out, fell asleep. I woke up with someone kissing me. I think I might have been dreaming about us, and then it was like the dream came true, and I thought your grandmother was better and you'd come up to surprise me."

I tried to figure out her expression, but she was in the shadows, and what I could see wasn't showing much. She didn't say anything, and she was still here, so I continued.

"She asked if I had a condom, and then I knew it wasn't you. I freaked."

Had I ever.

"Cooper said you screamed."

I shrugged. "I was still pretty drunk. Whatever I did brought a bunch of guys up to my room and scared the girl. I knew I needed to tell you before you heard it from anyone else. The guys said no one would tell you, but I had to be honest. We'd promised we would be."

Faith had insisted that if I didn't want to be with her, if I didn't want to do long-distance dating, I should tell her. She'd rather hear something from me than find out I'd been like her dad. No wonder she hadn't wanted to speak to me.

"The guys took my phone, but I found another one. I don't even remember exactly what I said, but it came out wrong, obviously. When I tried to call back and couldn't get an answer, I realized I'd messed up."

"There were a lot of sorrys, a didn't mean to, and mention of a bed and condom. It didn't paint a good picture."

There wasn't a good picture to paint, but it wasn't the one she'd seen. It hadn't been *that* bad. I couldn't read her voice. Was she still mad? Relieved? I couldn't tell.

"I'm sorry I didn't explain it better. It must have been horrible to hear that and think something had happened." I knew the way her dad cheated and the weird way her home was as a result. I'd never wanted to add that to her pain.

She sighed. "I don't know if I should apologize for not listening to you, but the way it sounded… I wasn't ever going to accept that. I knew the long-distance thing was a bad idea."

I opened my mouth, the words were right there, ready to blurt out. I hadn't messed up at long-distance dating. It had been a misunderstanding.

But I'd broken up with Holly before the summer. I wouldn't try long distance with her, even though I knew Faith and I had been broken up before we'd really had a chance to try it.

If Faith and I hadn't been separated by distance, I wouldn't have fallen asleep drunk because I was missing her. If there'd been a problem, I'd have talked to Faith in person, and I'd have explained everything. We wouldn't have had this misunderstanding. So maybe she was right about long distance?

Fuck. I had no idea.

"I'm sorry I've believed you did that all this time when you didn't. I just... If you'd really done that, I couldn't let you try to talk me around it. You get that, right? The way my dad always does with my mom?"

"I understand." And I did. I'd never been around when those uncomfortable talks happened, but Faith had overheard some of her parents' fights, and her mother had, in my opinion, over-shared with her daughter. It's why I'd always known I had no chance to explain to her. Maybe Cooper had really done me a favor tonight.

She pulled on her hair, something she did when she was nervous.

"I have no idea what we're supposed to do now."

I didn't, either.

"I know you think I'm wrong, but I don't think we'd have made it through the year," she said. "Being apart was going to be a problem. And now, well, we've both moved on. I know you have a girlfriend, and I respect that."

Shit. I couldn't say I was about to break up with Holly. It would sound sketchy as hell. But did I want to be with Faith again? I didn't know. A lot had happened this year. But I'd missed her. And I didn't want to walk around ignoring her or trying to avoid her. If nothing else, the team would give me shit about that. Cooper would, anyway.

"Maybe we could be friends?"

It was lame, asking a girl to be my friend. Like we were in grade school. But with all the history we had, it felt like the right call. We'd started as friends, and that had been a big part of our whole relationship. Faith was smart and loyal and understood hockey, which had been the thing we'd talked about most.

Maybe what I needed was just some time not dating anyone. Maybe with Faith as a friend, along with my team, it would be enough for a while. And after I figured out what I was going to do with hockey, I could figure out what I was going to do about dating and relationships. But there was a voice in my head saying maybe if Faith and I were friends again, something might happen. I called that the asshole part of my brain.

But even if nothing happened between us, the idea of having Faith around to hang with, talk hockey with—it eased a bit of the tension I carried around. I had time to think, because it took her a while to respond.

"Okay, friends. We'll see how that goes."

I held out a hand. "Shake on it?"

Her hand met mine, gave me a firm grip. "Happy?"

I was. I hadn't understood how much the Faith problem had bothered me until we cleared the air and agreed to be friends. It was like a big weight had been taken out of a backpack I was carrying around. I still had lots in there, but I felt lighter. And that felt good.

Then I remembered Holly. I had to go back into the house, get my girlfriend, and go break up with her. Yeah, that was going to be a shitty way to end the day.

Faith

I let Seb go back into the house. He did have a girlfriend there, after all. I needed a minute to think over what had just happened. I felt…a little freaked out, and a little like I'd just got new goalie equipment. Things weren't fitting quite right.

For a year, I'd been living with the knowledge that my long-time boyfriend had cheated on me almost as soon as he left for school. It had affected me in ways I hadn't considered until now, and I had to change my memories and a year's worth of thoughts. Cooper was right, it had made me question myself and my worth. My judgement. Now, I had to readjust my thinking. It was a lot easier to accept the bad opinions rather than the good ones.

It was going to take some time to make that adjustment. I wasn't going to get very far here in the backyard of women's hockey house during a party.

I had two options—leave the party and go home and think about all this or go in and enjoy myself at my team's party. I decided to go in and try to get this new equipment feeling like mine again. Break it in so that it fit. I was in college, I'd played a kick-ass game tonight, and I might have a few problems, but I'd just fixed one. I was ready to tackle more now.

Party it was.

7

Faith

I enjoyed the party. But my problems were still looming large when Monday rolled around. I spent the next couple of weeks before the start of the season working my butt off on the ice. I got some playing time in our exhibition games, but Coach Cray was still eyeing me with suspicion.

I attempted to get a head start on my classes. It wouldn't be easy to study on buses while we travelled, so I tried to get a bunch done now. I struggled. It was all just more, more than high school had been. I'd been an okay student in high school, but not a genius.

It came to a head one otherwise beautiful day. I got a D on a psych paper, so it was already a shitty day. Then I got the email with the roster for the first game of the season. I was walking back to my room from practice when my phone buzzed. I stepped off the sidewalk and opened the email to find out I wasn't starting. I'd expected that, but I wasn't even suiting up as backup. I slid down the tree trunk at my back and dropped my head on my knees. I had to wonder if I'd made the worse decision of my life coming to Burlington.

"Faith?"

Well, at least seeing Seb wasn't going to ruin my day. The email had already done that. I looked up at him. The weather had started to turn chilly, and the leaves were turning. The sun backlit him. He was alone, no girlfriend, in jeans and a T-shirt under his hockey jacket, looking like the guy I'd known before Moo U. The guy I'd have told all my problems to. Usually, he'd just listen to me. I'd told him early on that I'd ask for advice when I needed it. He'd listen, wrap his arms around me, and things didn't feel so bad. But we weren't those people anymore.

This year apart had changed me, and it must have changed him. Just like, when I really looked at him, he wasn't the same. He was bigger. He must have grown another inch or two. And he was more built. He also stood taller, more confidently. Grown up inside and out.

He'd be difficult to dislodge from the puck. It would be fun to watch him in a game. Wait, I had. From my goalie crease. And that just reminded me that no one was going to watch me play. I wanted to bury my head again and pretend, for a while, that this wasn't my life. But he was staring at me, and we'd agreed to be friendly, so I had to speak.

"Seb."

"You okay?"

I shrugged. He wasn't the guy I dumped my problems on anymore. Seb's eyes narrowed. Then he dropped to the ground beside me.

"Okay, what's wrong?"

"Who says anything's wrong?"

He rolled his eyes. "Faith, I know you. Something's bugging you."

I shook my head. I saw him stiffen, and he looked away.

"I thought we were going to be friends, but if this isn't something you want to talk about, okay, I'll respect that. Didn't mean to overstep."

I drew in a breath. My first response with him was anger, and I had to remind myself that I wasn't angry with him anymore.

"Sorry. I can share. There's nothing you can do about it though. I got a D, and I'm not playing in our first game, not even as backup. Just a shitty day."

He watched me, the familiar brown eyes checking my expression, my body language. He used to do that to see if I was hurting after a game but refusing to tell him. I'd never been good at hiding how I felt from him. He relaxed, so he must have decided I was telling the truth. I was.

"Who's starting the game?"

"Anders. Claire Anderson."

"She's a senior, right?"

I nodded. "Vashton's her backup. I'm not dressing."

He frowned. "What the hell, Faith? You're the best goalie on the team. Why aren't you at least on the bench?"

"Coach Cray hates me."

"Not possible. Your coaches always love you. You're the hardest working player on the ice, and you always made them look good."

I lifted a shoulder. "I still am, or one of them. But Coach has had it out for me since the first day on the ice. The freshman thing. Cooper asked me to stop some shots for your freshmen, and Coach decided I wanted to play on the men's team and not the women's team. She's still pissed about it."

Seb stretched out his legs on the grass. His nose scrunched up as he ran a hand through his hair, knee jiggling. "Sorry, Faith, that's my fault."

"What? You weren't even there—" I stopped, because he had been there. I hadn't seen him in the stands, but we'd bumped into each other in the hallway after.

Nope, that was still staying in the box. Seb might not be the cheating scumbag I'd believed he was, but he was still not my Seb. He had a girlfriend, and I'd just leave that whole encounter safely buried.

"I saw you on the ice and said something. Your name, I think. The guys asked how I knew you, and I didn't want to say you were the girl from last year. So I said you'd stopped shots for the Mav's. Remember? That was my first day on the team."

Of course, I remembered. It was how we'd met. The Mav's had brought me in to show up their new recruits. I'd done it the previous season, and you could learn a lot from how guys responded when they were beaten by a girl. The assholes pitched fits, made up excuses, and got angry. Seb hadn't. He'd stopped to tell me I'd done well. Smiled at me. Then we'd found out his billet family was in the house next to mine, and that's how it had all begun. Of course, Seb had told his teammates. I couldn't believe I hadn't connected those dots.

"I should have figured that out. I was pretty surprised when Blondie called me over and suggested the rookies shoot on me."

"Blondie?"

I grinned. "That's what I called Cooper the first time I saw him."

Seb laughed. "I like that."

I felt a full smile slip across my face. Seb had always made me happy. But then I remembered I didn't have a lot to be happy about.

Seb looked over at me. "Would you like me to talk to Coach Keller, explain what happened, and ask him to talk to Coach Cray?"

My smile vanished. "You're not serious, are you?"

Seb gave me that wary look, head still, only moving his eyes.

"Seb, there's a lot of competition between the men's and women's teams. Our workout time last week was cancelled because your team needed the space. You guys have the home locker room, right? With your own stalls and names? We have the guest one. So we can't claim stalls and have to move our gear out after games and practices.

"Coach Cray already thinks I would rather play with the men's team. Having your coach come to talk to her about me? I might as well quit the team immediately."

Seb studied my face. "I didn't know any of that."

"Well, why would you?"

He stared over the lawn, slowly shaking his head. "I feel kinda stupid."

I gave him a shove with my hand. "Yeah, you look it, too."

That brought his grin back to me. "Who're you calling stupid, stupid?"

This was where I was supposed to grin back and keep up the incredibly stupid insult trading. We'd done this a lot. But right now, that D on my paper said one of us was stupid, and I wasn't looking at him. I sighed.

"Wait, what's that face for? I didn't mean it, you know that."

It was still a shittastic day, even though goofing with Seb had made me forget that for a bit.

"I got a D on my first psych paper. I feel like stupid isn't far off the mark."

Next thing, Seb's arm was wrapped around me, pulling me in and feeling way too good. Way too familiar. But for a few minutes, I took that comfort. I needed it.

"You're not stupid, Faith. You've never been stupid."

He pulled back, removing his arm, and I did not almost whimper.

"Who's your prof? What class is it?"

"Warner. Intro to Psych. It's not anything related to what I want to major in, but I needed to clear out some of the required courses."

"I took that course with her. Maybe I could help you." He tilted his head, waiting to see if I'd jump at the offer of help.

"What grade did you get?" I was going to need a lot of help, and if he'd just scraped by…

He twisted his lips. "A."

"What? You got an A with Warner? A couple of my teammates told me she's really hard."

He shrugged and looked away. "I liked the class. I think I'm going to major in psych."

Things *had* changed this past year. I wanted to ask him why, but I wasn't sure I could ask something that personal. Not now. This was the first conversation we'd had since "the talk" after the exhibition game party. The second conversation in a year. We still had to work out what being friends would be like.

"So do you want my help?"

I bit my lip. I hated asking for help, but I needed it, and Seb was apparently a psych wiz. I couldn't do anything about my coach right now, and it would be nice to get a handle on something this year.

But that hug... Was I a little too happy about that?

"Come on, Faith. It's my fault you're in trouble with your coach, so let me do something to make up for that."

Okay, I needed the help, and I didn't know who else to ask for it.

Seb rose to his feet. "Come over to the hockey house. I'll hunt up my paper, and we can look over what Warner said about yours."

He held out a hand, and without thinking, I let him pull me up. I ended up a little too close to him, closer than friends would face each other. Close enough to bring back memories that I had no business indulging in. I took a quick step back. Just friends. Seb had a girlfriend, and I didn't want any distractions, especially not now.

I bent down to grab my backpack. "Okay, buddy. Lead the way."

Sebastien

One thing about living in the hockey house was you never knew what you were going to find when you got there. I didn't have to worry about Faith though. She was used to guys being idiots. One of the boys' teams she'd played on had thought it would be funny if they all simultaneously flashed her. She asked if they'd like her to rank their dicks, and if she should grade on a curve. They didn't try anything like that again. Especially when she muttered they were all below average.

When I opened the door and stood back to let her in, I could see we weren't going to be working in the living room. Cooper was planking on the coffee table with a bunch of solo cups balanced on his back, and Vonne was counting time.

"Devereaux!" Coop yelled.

"Five minutes," Vonne warned him.

"Blondie!" Faith called back. "Are you ticklish?" She took a step toward him.

"Not now. We've got a bet on."

Of course, they did. Cooper shot Faith a warning glance, his body tightening up in anticipation. Apparently, somebody *was* a little ticklish. Faith grinned, gave them a thumbs-up, and then followed me up the stairs. I opened the door to my room and went in. She paused in the doorway.

"You can come in."

I looked around. The room was pretty good. I was always tidy. Since I'd moved around a lot as a kid, I didn't collect much stuff. I kept things put away because I didn't want to be a problem. I'd seen some of my roommates living spaces. Hazardous. I could do what I wanted in this room, but the habits of a lifetime don't change easily.

"Are you sure this is okay?"

Was she worried we had a no-girls rule for our rooms? Hardly. I could only imagine the number of women who'd gone through Cooper's room, for example.

"Yeah. It's fine. I have no idea what the guys are up to down there, and I thought this would be a little quieter. We can leave the door open, if that's making you nervous."

We used to close the doors to our rooms and even lock them back when we were together. It had been our chance to make out or have sex. We'd been careful since we'd have been in trouble if we'd been caught. I couldn't imagine why Faith would be worried about that now. Unless it tied back to her coach somehow?

She stepped in and left the door open. "I just thought your girlfriend might not like it if you had someone in your room."

Oh. That.

"That girl is your girlfriend, right? The one at the party?"

I had to fess up, but I wasn't sure how Faith would take it. "She was."

She blinked, surprise on her face.

"I'm sorry. I didn't know you broke up."

I shrugged. "It was a couple of weeks ago."

Faith played with her braid, watching my face. "Do I say sorry or good riddance?"

I snorted. "Neither. She's a nice person. It just didn't work out." And that was on me.

I'd known at the party that it was time to end things between us. I was quiet for the rest of the party, and when people started to leave, I asked Holly if she was ready to head out. She'd looked at me for a moment, probably wondering what the problem was. I didn't ask her to come up to my room. I was waiting to end things, so I wasn't chatty. We walked across campus, and I was relieved that no one was hanging around the entrance to her res.

She turned to face me. "Do you want to talk here or in my room?"

I didn't want to go to her room. I took a breath. "I think we should break up."

She didn't say anything.

I was relieved I got that out there, and she didn't make a fuss. Maybe she'd guessed what was coming? I'd like to say she might have been ready to break up, too, but that talk she'd given me at the party wasn't a let's-break-up conversation. The silence stretched, making me uncomfortable.

"I don't think it's working, and I have to spend a lot of time on hockey right now," I said, filling in the lack of response from her. I thought she'd say *something*.

"Is it her?"

I could have played dumb, but I preferred to be honest. I

mean, I didn't want to say I was breaking up with her because I thought she only wanted to be with me because I played hockey. That was maybe too honest, and she might not even realize she was thinking that way. Maybe she wasn't. But I still felt antsy that she'd said cheating wasn't a deal breaker for her. I didn't want someone who was jealous and double-checking my every move, but if the idea of my cheating didn't upset her, how much did she really care? Still, since I knew she was asking about Faith, I answered her honestly about that.

"No."

Faith might have messed me up a bit by showing up, but I'd known this was what I was going to do before I even talked to Faith.

"Really? You ex shows and suddenly you want to break up?" There was anger in her voice now.

I huffed a breath in frustration. Guess I'd been too quick to think we could do this without the drama. "I'm not doing this because I want to ask Faith out. And she doesn't want to be with me."

I wanted to throw myself into hockey. Not be with someone who didn't know the real me, and not be with someone who knew me so well that breaking up took months to get over her.

Cooper was probably a lot smarter than I'd given him credit for.

Holly's arms were crossed. She shrugged. "I guess that's it. If you don't want to be with me, then we're done. But here's a tip, she thought you cheated once. She'll never get over that." She spun around and vanished into her dorm.

That last comment stung. I didn't see a future with Faith, not like we'd been. But knowing that a stupid misunderstanding would always mess with both of us? That was frustrating.

And now, here in my room, Faith was asking what happened with Holly, and I didn't know what to say. I tried for honest, because that was always how we'd been together.

"She wanted to be with a hockey player."

Faith's brows lifted. "Well, you are a hockey player."

"Yeah, but it would've been nice if she'd wanted to be with *this* hockey player."

Faith didn't say anything for a moment. "Sorry." She knew what I meant because of her dad's job. Women who hooked up with athletes because they were athletes. Women who married athletes because they were athletes. Even women who got pregnant to have a fixed income from a professional athlete. Her dad dealt with that kind of thing all the time as an agent.

I'd always wondered if he exclusively represented assholes, because it seemed like every one of his clients had something like that going on.

"Anyway," I said, not wanting to continue this conversation any longer, "I'll look up my stuff from last year with Warner in psych. Get your paper, and we'll see if we can make things better."

I was a lot more comfortable helping Faith with my best subject than applying the things I was studying in psych to my own life.

8

Faith

It was embarrassing how badly I'd half-assed the assignment. Seb gave me a few raised eyebrows and even an eyeroll, but he didn't say anything. Somehow, even though we'd started with me on his chair and him on his bed, we ended up on the bed together, backs against the wall, peering at his computer screen.

"You're good at this," I said when I'd had enough that my brain was frying.

He smiled, happy with the compliment. "I told you I was thinking of majoring in psych. I like it."

I leaned back and let my eyes run over him. "Hmmm. I think you would be good at stuff like counselling or advising, or whatever you do as a psych major."

"Really?"

I nodded but didn't say a lot more. Seb would be good at it because he was good at watching people and figuring them out. But the reason he was so good at it was because his parents were shitty. Not abusive, controlling kind of shitty. More like forgetful, unaware shitty.

Not everyone knew his story. I did because we'd been together so long. His parents had married because they'd gotten pregnant and had Seb. Then they'd found out they didn't really like each other, got divorced, and remarried before a lot of time had passed. They each had nice shiny new families, and Seb... Well, he was in the way. A reminder of a previous mistake. They didn't actively neglect him. They forgot him, showed too much relief when he was leaving, and none when he was with them. I'd seen them at a few of his games, and they'd looked like they couldn't wait to leave. They didn't know what to say to him. If I'd thought it would have done any good, I'd have talked to them.

Or maybe yelled at them.

The good part, for Seb, was that he got to go to hockey camps a lot, and it had made him a better player. He loved hockey, even though his family didn't. He'd never really belonged. When I heard they'd turned his room into a guestroom and put all his stuff in storage in the basement between visits, I wanted to wale on them. Seb had shrugged, but I knew it had hurt him.

Seb was always watching, trying to understand his family and other people around him so he could do whatever would help him fit in. His hockey team had become his real family. My home was shitty for different reasons, and for a while, we'd been family for each other.

I should give being friends with Seb a chance. A real chance. He was a good guy. When I thought he'd cheated, I'd been hurt and cut him off, but it had seemed odd he would do something like that when I'd always thought he was a decent person. I wouldn't have been willing to try long distance with anyone else.

Cooper showed up in the doorway, looking at the two of us sitting on the bed and smirking. "We were going to order pizza. You two in?"

I looked at Seb, and he cocked his head.

"Sure," he told Cooper. Question asked and answered between us with a look. That's what two years of dating did.

Cooper turned to go back down the stairs. I started to slide off the bed, grabbing the embarrassing paper to put in my backpack. Seb stood up and headed for the door.

"I'll grab Cooper before they order to make sure one pizza doesn't have mushrooms. He loves them and puts them on every pizza if someone doesn't stop him."

I smiled up at him from my position squatting on the floor. That knowledge, about how much I hated fungi, also came from being as close as we had.

"Thanks."

Sebastien

I gave Cooper a shove when I got to the kitchen. "At least one of those pizzas better not have mushrooms on it. Faith hates mushrooms."

Cooper turned with a big grin. "I bet you didn't even have to ask her what she wanted."

"No, because we've had a lot of pizza together. We dated for almost two years, idiot."

"You two looked pretty cozy up there."

I held my hands up in a T.

"Timeout, Coop. I need you to be serious."

Cooper could be a brat, but he knew when to turn it off. "What is it, Hunter?"

"Faith and I are just friends. Don't mess that up for me."

He watched me for a minute, expression serious. "Okay. Welcome to Team Single. Ready to have fun?"

"Right now, I'm ready for pizza. Just leave the rest."

He shrugged and called the pizza place.

Faith fit in like she'd been here with us before. We ate pizza, played some video games, and talked hockey. Faith called Cooper Blondie, to the amusement of the rest of the guys in the house. It was nine o'clock when she checked the time and said she had to go.

"Turning into a pumpkin, Dev?" Cooper asked.

"No, Blondie, just gotta do some reading and get up early for class."

Cooper shook his head. "Freshman mistake. Don't take those early classes."

Faith threw a pillow at him. "Nice for you guys. You have afternoon practice. Ours has to be over before you start, so our schedules get fucked up."

Cooper looked surprised. Yeah, that hadn't occurred to me either until Faith had talked about the conflicts between the teams. But she was shoving on her shoes at the door, so I followed her.

"I'll walk you."

She nudged me with her shoulder. "I'm good."

"I'll walk you."

Moo U was pretty safe, but no place was a hundred percent safe, especially for women. Plus, I was enjoying hanging out with her. If we hadn't been friends first, I don't think we'd have dated so long. The air was cool, and the stars were bright. We walked in relative quiet. There were only a few students out at this time of night. I didn't know where Faith was staying, but now I would.

I was glad I'd seen her under that tree. I wanted to do the friends thing. We got to her res. One of the WE ones. I bet her dad was behind that.

"Thanks for the walk, Seb." She turned to open the door of her building.

"Just a sec."

She turned back.

"We're friends now, right?"

She nodded. "Yeah, friends."

"Can I have your number then?"

Faith had blocked me last year when she'd thought I cheated. I understood why, but surely we were okay to call or text now? If she gave me her number, I would know we were past what had happened, that she believed what I'd told her.

She pulled out her phone. She was smiling. "Absolutely."

I was more relieved than I probably should have been.

Warner is a sadist

Look at U, using psych terms

Yeah, not gonna help me with this next paper

Want help from a friend who already aced this class?

I can buy U lunch to pay for picking Ur brain

Great game last night.

Yeah, we did pretty well. Sorry U didn't get ice time.

I got to dress for the game, which is a step up

U need to talk to your coach, fix things

Or I could totally piss her off by saying the wrong thing and never get on the ice again

Still feel bad about that

I just can't believe it would piss her off that much

I never realized how much harder it was 4 the women's team and now I feel like we're all assholes

Not all of U

Blondie okay after that hit?

Fucking asshole should have got a game misconduct. Coop is fine just not as pretty

That was quite the hit you gave him afterward

Fucking asshole

Does that mean the two of u aren't going to be besties?

Did I leave my biology book in ur room last night?

I'll check

No but it was in the living room.

Right, it must have fallen out of my backpack while we were playing video games.

Can U bring it 2 the coffeehouse?

This aft when we're meeting up, or do U need it before then?

Why don't we meet up there now? Then U don't have to carry it around all day

On my way

———

Did I leave my scarf in your room? I can't find it anywhere

It's not in my room, let me check the living space

How the hell did it get under a couch cushion?

Hell if I know. I didn't even sit there yesterday. Penny and her boyfriend were using it, remember?

Gremlins, obvs.

I'll come by for it before lunch. We're catching a bus at 2 for Massachusetts

I'm at practice then. I'll bring it with me

K

———

Faith

"Thanks for bringing this, Faith."

I'd stepped off the ice to grab the scarf for him from the bench where I'd left it. We were at practice, but Coach was focused on the forwards for the moment.

"Is the temperature about to plunge, or something?" I had no idea why Seb wanted the scarf. It wasn't cold out yet. It was a Moo U one, so he must've gotten it last year.

His cheeks flushed. Something was up.

"Fess up, Seb. What is it?"

He looked around the arena. "It's, my, um…lucky scarf."

I laughed, like he knew I would. He didn't get mad. He just pulled at the hair ribbon on my braid. "And this is…"

I jerked back, pulling the braid out of his grasp.

"Yes, it's my lucky ribbon, but I actually need to wear it while I'm playing. You want to tell me you stuff that inside your pads somewhere while you're on the ice?"

He tucked the scarf in his jacket pocket, green spilling out because it didn't fit. "The day I got this, I had my first decent game for the Bulls and scored two assists."

Burlington's teams were called the Bulls. Technically, we on the women's team were also Bulls. I had a hard time keeping my face straight at the thought of it. Obviously, the name had been chosen by some male founder who didn't think women would one day compete since their vaginas would probably fall out if they tried. I hoped that asshole could see us now.

I wondered if someone had given that scarf to Seb, maybe a girlfriend, but I didn't ask. That crossed a line. We were friends, but not the way we were before. I wasn't really sure I wanted to know who'd given him the scarf.

"You gonna practice with us, Devereaux?"

Shit. Coach Cray. And that tone in her voice was not a happy you're-doing-great tone.

"Yes, Coach." I turned to wave goodbye to Seb. I hoped she wouldn't make a big deal of this, but I could just see the ideas in her head. Me, trying to get tight with the men's team and its players.

She narrowed her eyes as she looked at Seb.

"You're Hunter. Defenseman on the men's team."

Seb nodded. "Faith brought me something I'd left behind. Our bus is about to leave."

Cray arched her brows. "Friends, are you?"

I could see this further convincing her I wasn't interested in her team. *Shit.*

Seb gave her a polite smile. "We go way back. I was billeted at her neighbor's house when I was a Junior in Toronto."

Coach's brows came down. I was grateful Seb had defused things, making us sound like old buddies. Just buddies. So old that it would be rude not to be friends. Which we kind of were, but also more.

Seb didn't stop there. "Yeah, I met her when I joined my Junior team. The other guys on the team had us all face off against Faith in net. Even back then, she stopped everyone. So it's my fault she did that here on her first day. I mentioned it to a teammate, and well, he couldn't let that go. We're all about twelve mentally." He shot me a glance, and I sent him back a what-the-fuck one. I'd hoped the coach would forget that incident.

He kept his polite smile in place. "Thanks, Faith. Good luck this weekend, Coach Cray."

He turned to go, and I shot Coach a quick glance before I turned to rejoin practice. She looked more thoughtful than pissed. Anything was better than pissed.

Saturday night, I got my first start.

Sebastien

When I read the text from Faith that she was scheduled to start, my knees got a little weak. I wasn't sure if I'd made things worse with her coach, but it had been riding me that she'd gotten on her coach's bad side because of something stupid I'd said.

Saturday, I was distracted for our own game simply because I wanted to know how she was doing. I knew she was good, but she hadn't played in a real game for a while. It was different. We could all practice and work out endlessly, but that didn't translate into playing well in a game. Not practicing and working out would leave us playing like shit, but games were different. And it meant too much to me that Faith did well.

I checked on the score after our first period. Cooper noticed, because of course he did.

"What's bugging you, Hunts? You were out of position twice on our first shift."

Cooper and I had been paired together, as we'd expected. We were the second line but still getting a lot of minutes. I wasn't a big scoring threat, but I was always solid. Being out of position was not something I did. Before tonight, we'd been playing well, and I shouldn't have let myself get distracted.

I might as well tell him before he tried to figure it out on his own. He was smart, and he didn't give up. Great for a hockey player, not so great when you wanted to keep something from him.

"Faith is playing tonight. First game this season."

He watched me carefully. "Worried about your buddy?"

I nodded. Their first period had been scoreless, and Faith had stopped ten shots. That was good. I just wished her forwards had done something to help her out.

Coop dropped down on the bench beside me. "So how's she doing?"

"Scoreless first. She stopped ten shots."

"That's pretty good. How many shots did we have this period?"

I opened my mouth but couldn't answer.

Cooper shook his head. "When are you two going to admit you're more than friends? It's not like I'm the relationship guru, and even I can see it."

I felt blood rushing to my cheeks and wanted to punch Cooper. I didn't need him digging around in my head. The phrase ignorance was bliss? I was a fan of that one.

"She's not interested, Cooper."

He shrugged. "I call it as I see it."

"Yeah, well, you don't see everything. You don't know her story."

He didn't answer. He looked at me for a moment and then

shrugged. "Well, try to get your head into our game, because we need a win, too."

We got our win, and I did manage to keep my focus on our game for the last two periods. I still checked the women's scores after each period and was just as happy that Faith got her win. Not a shutout, and I knew I'd hear her moan about that for a day or two until she let it go.

I tamped down Cooper's comment in my head. Faith and I were friends, and I wasn't going to do anything to mess that up. Faith trusted me now, but as a friend. I didn't know if I would ever convince her to try dating me again, certainly not now. Now, we were still building trust. I couldn't even let my mind consider whether my feelings for Faith were crossing that line. I needed plausible deniability. Fuck Cooper and his calling it as he saw it.

I needed to keep my libido under control. I was just out of a relationship with Holly. It would be too messed up to rush into asking Faith to try again. I'd told Holly I didn't break up with her because of Faith. I didn't want to be a liar. I wasn't sure if I wanted more with Faith, but I didn't want to lose what we had now. It was easier not to think about it, because then I couldn't ask for more than I could get.

9

Faith

Life had improved. And if I was totally honest, a lot of that had to do with Seb. I couldn't say for sure that what he'd said to Coach had changed her mind about that first day. But I was getting to start every other weekend. I knew I was playing well. My teammates knew it too and were happy.

The other freshman goalie, Vash, was my roommate on the road, and we spent a lot of time together. I knew I was better than she was, but for the team to do well, she had to improve. I spent time working with her at practices, above and beyond what our coach did with us, and I think that helped Coach Cray's opinion of me as well.

I wasn't being altruistic or trying to impress Coach. If our team were to get to the playoffs, we all had to be at our best. If Anders or I went down, Vash would need to step up. Every game might affect our position in the playoffs at the end of the season, so it was only smart to make sure she could fill in when needed. Vash herself hadn't warmed up to me, but right now I needed to focus on my relationship with Coach Cray.

School was finally making some sense. Seb had helped with that. He'd helped a lot with Professor Warner, and somehow, learning to do well with her had translated into my other classes as well.

My roommate, Penny, was still working on my makeover. After that first party where I'd let her choose my clothes and do my makeup, she'd decided I was now her project. I didn't think I needed a makeover, necessarily, but I did like exploring more girlie things—clothes and makeup, which was what Penny was into. I'd never had a girlfriend like her before. We spent time together when I wasn't away at games or practicing, and she wasn't busy with friends. The cross-country guy hadn't lasted, but now she'd found a basketball player.

I was bonding with my team and hanging out with Seb a lot. I finally felt that college was going the way it was supposed to. Like it did in the movies or on TV. I played on the weekend and recorded my first shutout against a good team. I'd gotten a B on a psych paper this morning, and Seb insisted we needed to go out for pizza to celebrate. I was on board for that. Living in the WE res meant that I normally followed a strict eating plan. I knew that was good for me, but once in a while, I could afford to break the diet. I'd had pizza at the hockey house, drank a bit at the occasional party, and I was still playing at my best. I could handle some Tito's pizza.

I was almost ready to go. Penny was critiquing what I looked like even though this was only pizza with Seb when my mom called. Penny's basketball player was coming over, so I grabbed my coat and stepped out of the room, heading down to meet Seb while answering the call.

"Hey, Mom, what's up?"

I stopped moving when she told me.

Sebastien

I got to Faith's residence a little early, looking forward to pizza and time with Faith. We hung out all the time now, but not usually just the two of us. Her roommate was around if we were at Faith's dorm, and the hockey house was always packed with people. Unsurprisingly, Faith got along well with the guys. She was friends with all of them and would tease them, play video games with them, and dissect our games with them. It was a gang hang, unless there was a party somewhere else, and then we were with the guys at that party. The team didn't go out a lot. We kept things under control enough to play well. It was all about balance. Coach would probably balance the scales a little further away from the party side, but as long as we were playing as well as we were, he didn't ask questions, and we didn't tell.

I was enjoying the year the way I'd hoped I would. And now that Faith had shown up and we had cleared the air between us, it was even better. Except for the girlfriend part. But it was probably good that I was single for a bit. I hadn't met anyone who'd made me want to change my status since Holly.

"When are you two going to admit you're more than friends?"

I'd been trying to forget Cooper's words, but they popped up every now and then. Faith had agreed to being friends, so I was being the best friend I could be with her. I didn't get to see her on weekends, because when we had home games, her team was away. And when she was home to play, we were away. That took care of weekends together until December, since we didn't have any breaks in our schedule.

If we didn't travel far, whichever team was on the bus would get back on Saturday night and be free on Sundays. Faith and I would get together then to study or play or just hang out. And we had weekday evenings. And sometimes lunch. Basically, anytime we could make it work.

If Faith gave a single sign she was up for more, I suspected I'd have her in my arms without a second thought. So much for plausible deniability. Cooper had blown that. I just couldn't risk what we did have. She was my best friend. She knew my shitty family history, and I knew hers. We shared a love of hockey, which right now took up almost all our free time. After two years of dating, we understood each other.

That was big for me.

Faith's friendship was a kind of security I'd never gotten from my own family. It had been hard feeling like I never had a place where I could be myself. I always had to be careful, make sure I didn't make waves, make sure I fit in without causing discomfort. It had never been enough to make me belong. When I'd joined the billet family and then Faith and I had started hanging out back in Toronto, I'd had my first real taste of belonging. It had taken time, but eventually I'd been able to be shitty around her. I realized I could get angry and pissed, and she wouldn't withdraw or leave. She'd just gotten pissed right back. And then we'd work it out, and I could relax. And we'd have sex.

I could be me, and Faith stayed.

I'd convinced Faith we could date long distance because I hadn't wanted to give that up. It hadn't been just about the sex, though that had been awesome. But the rest of it had been even more important. And that's why I wouldn't risk what we had now for any fuck, no matter how good. We were getting that back. It wasn't totally the same—we didn't talk much about last year— but we were almost there. I wouldn't risk pushing for romance when I might lose that feeling of belonging. So there was lots of me and my hand in the shower, but I could live with that. At least, for now.

Maybe just the two of us at dinner tonight would be the next step to getting back to everything we'd had before. I'd watch her, try to pick up clues. I was feeling optimistic for once. I sent her a text to say I was here.

Nothing.

I waited. Faith normally responded right away, but she could be in the bathroom or something. I called. Her line was busy. Someone came out the res door, so I caught it and started up. Faith wouldn't mind. I hoped she wouldn't.

Then my brain got busy with that underlying fear I never lost. I worried, trying to remember what could have happened since I last saw her to mess things up. The breakup last year had come out of nowhere. I immediately worried that something else had come up relating to that. Maybe that girl had found her, told a different story? Had someone told her I'd been with a girl somewhere this year? Taken a photo? Made her think I'd cheated on Holly?

She'd talk to me if so, wouldn't she?

I found her in the hallway frozen still. She didn't even notice me standing right in front of her. I could hear from the phone beeping that whoever had been on the other side of the call had hung up. Whatever she'd heard had upset her. So much that she hadn't pressed her off button.

Was it something about me?

I checked her expression. She was hurting. It hit me that I needed to help. I had a horrible vision of her wearing the same expression when I called in the stupid drunken fit of remorse last year. Had I done the same thing to her then? The thought made my stomach curl up. But that wasn't the situation now. Now it was something else, it had to be, and I needed to get my head out of the past and see what she needed. I put a hand on her wrist, the one still gripping her phone. That caught her attention, and she looked up at me, shock dilating her pupils.

"Seb."

It wasn't an accusation. Whatever had happened wasn't connected to me. We were still just friends. But Faith was hurting, so I wrapped my arms around her and pulled her into a hug. She needed that comfort. She was stiff for a moment, then she relaxed and clamped her arms around my waist. It felt good having her there. Probably too good, but I shoved the thought aside.

"It's my grandmother," she said into my jacket.

"I'm sorry." She only had one grandmother she was close to, the one who'd had a stroke a year ago. I was afraid this might be the worst news. It would devastate Faith. They were close, and she was a super nice lady.

"She's got cancer."

I felt that pain inside. I'd met the woman, and she was everything I would have liked in a grandmother.

"I'm sorry." I had nothing else to offer. Just my words and my arms around her.

"They're giving her just a few months."

"Oh, baby, I'm so sorry."

I was. Her grandmother had been a rock for Faith growing up. Her parents' marriage was volatile. Her dad cheated, her mother got upset, things were tense, they got counselling or something and pretended everything was fine. Until the next time her dad cheated. And there'd always been a next time.

Sometimes, her mom had traveled with Faith's dad, so he couldn't complain he was lonely or use some other stupid excuse for his indiscretions. When Faith was too young to be on her own, her grandparents had taken care of her. Her grandfather died about a year before I met her. Her grandmother had come to every game Faith played, unless it had been too far to drive. Until the stroke last year. Her grandmother had been going through therapy since then, was close to getting full functionality back. Faith told me about working with her until she'd come to Moo U. The two of them doing their workouts together. It wasn't fair that the woman had been hit with cancer now. I was upset to hear this news, and I wasn't Faith.

"You want to go back to your room?" I wasn't going to leave her, but we couldn't stand in the hall forever.

She shook her head. "Penny's there. I don't want to talk about it with her. Not yet."

Penny would say she was sorry and ask questions. Not that that was a bad thing, but Faith didn't want that right now. I was pretty sure she wanted to come to terms with it before anyone else asked about it. And she hated it when people saw her cry.

"Okay, my place it is. The guys went out. We'll order pizza in, and you can do whatever you need to."

Nothing like this had come up when we'd dated, so I didn't know if she'd want to cry, block it out, talk, or whatever.

Faith sniffed. "No, I don't want to mess up your evening. You go have fun. I'll be fine."

I pulled back from Faith far enough for her to see my face. "I'm not leaving my friend. And don't forget, I know your grandmother, so this upsets me, too, even though she's not my family. We can go back to my place, you can have time to get your game face back on, and I dunno, you want to buy plane tickets to fly back?"

"Gramma said I can't come back if I'm missing hockey. She said she'll beat this thing, but she doesn't want me to miss any games."

Faith's voice was tight, and I knew she was fighting tears. And she'd hate that I knew she was close to crying. She'd only cried about twice the whole time we'd dated.

"Well, how about we go to my place, you cry out whatever you need to, and then you can call her. Is that a good plan?"

She pulled me close again. "Thanks, Seb. That sounds good."

The guys were out, but I took her to my room. If she wanted to cry, I was going to give her privacy. There was no telling when someone would show up, and I didn't want them asking questions. I ordered pizza and grabbed some beer from our fridge. When I got back to my room, I closed the door.

Faith had curled up on the bed. My bed. I stepped over, passed her a beer, and sat down. I considered hugging her again, but getting that close on my bed might distract at least part of my brain, the asshole part, into thinking things that I shouldn't. So I kept a little distance.

"Do you wanna talk, or try not to think about it? We could watch something on my laptop."

She lifted her head, her rimmed-red eyes meeting mine. "I want to see her. I should have spent more time with her. When I see Coach tomorrow, I'm going to ask for some time off."

I settled beside her, back to the wall, legs stretched over the bed. Just enough distance between us.

"It's too bad she couldn't come here and watch you play again. I know she'd like that."

Faith pushed back her braid. "Could she do that?"

I stared at her. "Um, I don't know." I was a sophomore psych major. I did not know if stroke survivors with cancer could fly to watch a hockey game. I'd just been rambling, wanting to make Faith feel better. I must have done that. She sat up and had a hopeful expression.

"That's a great idea. I'll text my mom and see if she could do that."

I had no idea if her grandmother was up to travelling, but I was glad to see some life back in Faith's eyes. She texted back and forth with her mom for a while. I went and got the pizza when it arrived and brought it up.

"If Coach will let me know when I'm playing, they think they can come down for a weekend. Oh, pizza. Thanks!"

Maybe this plan wouldn't work out, but Faith had something to look forward to. She wasn't crying, and that was thanks to me, and that felt really good.

Faith

I felt lighter. There was still the knowledge that I was losing Gramma. She'd assured me she was going to fight it, but Mom had told me what the doctor said. I wanted to go home, to give up on the semester and stay with Gramma as long as I could. It was frustrating that she was so insistent I not do that.

She was proud of me for playing and had been the first person to tell me I could do this, that I could play in a men's professional league if I wanted. Win the Cup. She and Gramps had always been my biggest fans.

She wanted me to keep playing for her. Ironic that I could've gone home and seen her during the first part of the semester when I hadn't gotten time to play. But the idea of having her come and see me play again? It made me feel like crying, but good crying. And I was so grateful to Seb for thinking of it.

"Seb, thanks so much. For…all of this. I know you wanted to do something else—"

He shook his head. "No, this is fine. I mean, you just got news about your grandmother. Whatever you need."

And then the words hit home, and I threw myself against his chest and bawled. I wasn't proud of that. But it was sinking in, becoming real. Gramma was dying. Soon, not someday in the nebulous future. I don't know how long he let me stay there soaking his shirt while he rubbed my back and I cried like a kid. I cried my fear and my regret and my sorrow out in a stream of tears and snot. I finally slowed down to a sniffle. This was so hard. And so unfair. She was just about done recovering from her stroke.

Seb had been great. He knew Gramma, and he knew what she meant to me. He'd come up with this idea that might work, and then he'd let me cry on him. I'd needed a friend. One that knew me, really knew me. I was so glad we'd cleared up what had happened last year, and that I had him again.

"I don't think I'd have gotten through tonight without you." My voice was rough, and the words came out muffled, but he got the idea.

He tightened his arm, and I turned my face up, wanting to thank him, to maybe kiss his cheek. But I misjudged, or he moved, and my lips touched his. And suddenly, it was us again. The two of us, on a bed, with chemistry that burned way too hot for friends.

10

Faith

I clutched his shirt, and he pulled me into his lap. Our lips fused together, and I didn't know if I heard my moan or his. But our tongues were tangling, and I was reaching under his shirt, and my thoughts weren't sad any longer. They were R rated.

Seb pulled back, chest heaving. "Faith, are you sure?"

I realized I was a red-eyed, stuffed-up mess, but I wanted this. I wanted joy and pleasure and to forget the shitty stuff that was waiting for me when we left this room again.

"Please?"

He sat up and pulled off his shirt while I tugged at mine. I wrenched off my sports bra, and he closed his eyes for a moment. Then his hands were on my breasts, and his mouth slammed back on mine, and it was like the last year had never happened. We'd always gone from zero to sixty in seconds, at least for the first round.

Seb had been my first, and I'd been his. Since the first time we kissed, we'd worked out each step together, finding what worked for each of us. We knew each other's bodies intimately. He knew exactly how to touch my breasts to make me crazy, and I knew that biting on his nipples could almost push him over the edge. Especially if he was in me then.

We used all that knowledge to take us up to eleven as quickly as possible. He kissed under my ear and along my neck, which sent goosebumps racing over my skin. I ran my nails down his back, and he shivered, pressing his mouth harder into my skin. I dug my fingers in deeper, wanting him closer, touching more, kissing more, just more everything.

His hands, his mouth did more for me than anyone else had ever been able to do. I shoved that thought away and instead fumbled with his zipper as he slid his hands down the back of my pants, running them over my ass. He rolled over me, lifting his hips so I could shove down his jeans, mouth now moving on my breasts, pressing kisses, nipping, licking. Driving me crazy.

I said something intelligent like, "Unngh."

He pulled away and tugged on my waistband. I tilted my hips up, staring at him through heavy lids. His cheeks were flushed, his pupils wide. I loved seeing him like this, looking as turned on as I felt. He focused on the parts of me being revealed as he slid my jeans and panties down my legs and threw them heedlessly to the floor.

We were still for a moment, panting. Seb moved his gaze to mine. "You're sure? Please say you're sure."

I reached for his cock, gripping it the way I knew he liked.

"Thank fuck." He shivered as I stroked him, and he reached his hand between my legs.

I opened for him, needing his touch, needing that friction that would ratchet up my arousal and push me over the edge.

"You're so wet." He moaned, thrusting into my hand.

I slid my other hand past his, reaching under his balls to stroke the sensitive skin. He shuddered.

"How do you want to do this?" He dropped forward, arm braced by my head. He nuzzled my neck, nipping and licking where he knew it drove me crazy.

"I've got condoms."

He stopped moving. "But—"

"Non-latex. They're good."

He was still. I froze, too. This was different, not the way we'd been. We'd gone bare most of the time we'd been together. But that was then. He'd had girlfriends since, and I'd been with a couple of other guys. We couldn't pretend that hadn't happened. We couldn't go bare with that kind of trust, not now.

I took my hands off him and grabbed his face, making him look at me.

"I don't want to stop. Do you?"

He bit his lip and shook his head.

I sat up, twisted under his arm, and leaned down to my backpack.

There'd been a safe-sex talk at orientation, and they'd handed out condoms back at the beginning of the year. I'd offered mine to Penny since I couldn't use them. She'd insisted I put some of the ones I could use in my backpack. "Just in case," she'd said. I hadn't planned on sleeping with anyone, but it had been easier to put them there than to argue with her. Right now, I was awarding her points for roommate of the year. Because I had three non-latex condoms in a pocket inside my bag

I felt Seb's hand stroking my ass as I scrambled in my bag. I held up my prize with one hand. He reached for it, but I shook my head. "Let me."

He leaned back, pupils blown with arousal. I took a moment, reestablishing him in my memory. The muscled chest was bigger and heavier now. The dark hair across his pecs trailed down until it reached his cock. And his cock, which I'd touched and tasted and come on so often, was hard. So hard.

I shivered.

"Faith," he said, voice deep, and I ripped open the package, not wanting to wait any longer.

I didn't have a lot of experience with putting on condoms, but this was Seb. I'd learned everything I knew with him. He hissed when I reached to hold him with one hand and used the other to roll the condom down. He looked up again, waiting for me. Patient. It was one of his best assets on the ice. And here, too.

"Can I be on top?" I dropped a kiss on his lips. I needed that control. I was still a bag of emotional confusion, and this was so unexpected. I wanted to set the pace, take charge. He always let me.

He pressed a kiss to my stomach. "As long as I get inside you, you can do anything you want."

He stretched out on his back, and I straddled him, resting over his rock-hard erection, sliding back and forth, letting my wetness lubricate us both, while at the same time stimulating us more. I was shaking with need, but I took my time, watching his chest rise and fall, his cock hard beneath me. It felt familiar, safe, and the memories made me hotter. He reached for my breasts, stroking his thumbs over my nipples. I closed my eyes, shivering at the stimulation.

I lifted up and gripped him, placing him just right for me to slide down slowly. Clenching my core muscles to keep me in position, I took him in inch by inch. My eyes were closed again, enjoying the fullness, the friction, the warm arousal spreading like fire through my body. Seb was panting. He moved his hands down to my hips, clenching them, but he didn't pull me down. He let me set the pace. Once he was all the way in, we both groaned, overcome.

It was good. So, so good.

A part of me wanted to keep it slow, make it last, but that part of me was lost as he moved one sneaky finger and rubbed my clit. I could feel the orgasm just on the edge of my grasp. He thrust up, meeting me, those strong abs and thighs powering him as I slammed down, chasing the peak. I heard Seb, from a distance, saying, "Fuck, fuck, fuck," over and over. He'd never been much of a dirty talker.

He pressed on my clit again, and I growled his name as my orgasm took me. My vision blanked, my mind emptied, and I was nothing but waves of pleasure rippling through my body. I found myself collapsed on Seb's chest. His face and neck were flushed, and I could feel the twitches of his cock as he finished coming.

Inside me.

I let my eyes close again. I was limp and spent, unwilling to move. Seb's hands moved up my back, down, and then to my waist, sliding me off him, onto the bed.

Condom, my muzzy brain thought. He has to take care of the condom. And I should get up. But I needed a moment. I was exhausted from the tension of the evening, from my crying jag, and from the best orgasm I'd had since…

Since Seb.

Sebastien

My knees were still a little wobbly when I came back from the bathroom. I heard the guys downstairs slamming the door as they returned, so I kept as quiet as I could. Faith wouldn't want to answer a bunch of questions. I took a breath before I opened the door to my room again. I wasn't sure what I was going to see when I looked at Faith. If she regretted this, if I'd blown everything, I was going to punch myself. Repeatedly. I dreaded seeing her pulling on her clothes, refusing to meet my eyes. Ideally, she'd be still in my bed, eyes warm and soft, and maybe, if I was really lucky, ready to try round two.

Faith was there in my bed, right where I'd left her. But she wasn't looking for a repeat. She'd fallen asleep. I stood for a moment, wondering what I should do. Had she planned to spend the night here with me? Or had the day, with the news about her grandmother and the crying and the sex, just wiped her out? What was going to happen when she woke up? What did I want out of all this, once the sex thoughts settled down?

I wasn't sure.

I picked up our clothes from where they lay scattered around. I folded up hers and set them on the desk chair. Then I pulled out an old T-shirt of mine and put it on the end table near her head. If she was cold or worried about being naked, she could put it on. Of course, she might just dress and slip out.

I wished I knew where her head was at.

I watched her for a moment. Her braid was half unraveled, and the loose strands were framing her face. Her expression was relaxed in sleep, and I hoped she could remain like that a long time and stay unaware of what was happening with her grandmother. Her nose was pink, and there was red around her eyes from her crying. She'd wake up thirsty.

I could take care of that.

I pulled on sweatpants and slipped out of the room quietly, planning to get her a sports drink to leave by the bed. She might wake up and want to get out of the house as soon as she could, but at least I could make sure she'd be comfortable. That's what friends did. I had no idea if we were more than that now, or if the friendship was gone. I couldn't think about that or I'd be sick.

Cooper was in the kitchen, beer in one hand, frowning at his phone in the other one. He looked up and then raised his eyebrows.

"Well, well, well. Looks like someone is very relaxed."

I could feel heat in my cheeks. I looked down at my chest and saw red marks. Cooper was not going to believe those came from hockey practice.

I shrugged and opened the fridge. He could think what he wanted. I wouldn't mention Faith's name, and I would warn her, if I had the chance. We could find a way to sneak her out if we needed to.

"Those Faith's boots by the door?"

I closed my eyes, hand fisted around a sports drink. Fuck. I hadn't thought of that. I could say she'd left behind a jacket or hat if he'd spotted that, but how the hell would someone leave without footwear? Still, I could try to cover for her.

"Are you memorizing Faith's clothes now?" It was the best I

could come up with. She was going to be so pissed, and I didn't know what I could do about it.

Cooper rolled his eyes. "I don't have to. She's here so much we could almost charge her rent."

I turned around, drink in hand, mind racing for something to say. Cooper wasn't frowning at the phone any longer. Now his arms were crossed, beer dangling from the fingers of one hand.

"I'm glad if you two worked things out. And I won't tell if you don't want me to."

I leaned back against the fridge and sighed. I couldn't very well pretend now. And maybe, since he already knew, I could ask him for advice. Things were twisted if I was asking Coop.

"I don't know if we've worked anything out."

He nodded at my chest. "Looks like you worked something."

My cheeks were even warmer now. I stared up at the ceiling, not brave enough to look at him while I talked.

"Faith heard today that her grandmother has cancer. She only has a few months to live. We were supposed to get pizza at Tito's, but I brought her here, and she cried a bit, and…"

Cooper watched me, and from the corner of my eyes, I saw him nod.

"I get it. And after that?"

"She fell asleep. Just now."

"You didn't ask her to stay, or—"

I shook my head. "She crashed while I was in the bathroom." I didn't finish that sentence, and Coop nodded. He knew.

"When she wakes up?"

"No idea." I held up the bottle. "Was going to bring her this so she can hydrate."

"Always important." Cooper was still staring at me with his eyes narrowed, as if I were far away. "What about you? Did you want her to stay?"

I wanted to say yes. This was Faith. My best friend, and the best sex I'd ever had. We'd taught each other everything. I still cared for Faith. And after what we'd just done, my dick was ready to get right back to where we'd been before the stupid phone call that blew up our relationship. The rest of me? The rest of me was on board with that, too, except... Except I knew Faith. The fact that the two of us were here on the same campus meant the long-distance problem was gone.

The athlete problem was not.

Before, we'd often had away games at the same time, but now, any time her team played at home, my team was on the road. Every time, since our teams shared the arena. Back in Toronto, a lot of games, especially hers, had been local. Sometimes, when I'd been away and she hadn't had a game, she'd come to mine, and vice versa. Now, every weekend—Friday afternoon through late Saturday or even Sunday—we'd be apart. She'd worried about it before, and I thought I'd understood. There might be some girls interested in even a boring freshman defenseman. I was a sopho-more now, and with the ice time Cooper and I were getting, that number was rising. Would Faith be able to trust me? She'd certainly been quick to leap to the wrong conclusion last time. Probably with cause, since I'd been drunk and crying, but I'd had no chance to explain.

"When you're thinking that long, the answer isn't yes."

I shoved my hand through my hair. "It's not no. It's just—"

"If you say complicated, I'll give you a wedgie."

Right, like he had any idea of what complicated was like. One and done, no complications, no repeats, no problems. Still, he was a sounding board. Maybe he'd have something helpful to tell me. Despite my doubts, he'd certainly been instrumental in bringing Faith and I back together as friends.

"I've been happy being friends. I really have."

Cooper smirked. "Uh huh."

"I mean, we both moved on after..."

He pointed at me. "Was that what you were doing that got your chest marked up like that?"

I lifted my hands, as if to cover the marks, which was stupid, but stupid and I were familiar with each other. "Yeah, well, sex was never the problem with us."

Not sex between the two of us. Just the sex she thought I had with someone else. And the sex she'd had with her rebound. I wasn't in any place to talk, but still…

"So what's the problem? It's not as good as it is with other women?" He set his beer on the counter.

I frowned. "No, man. The sex is awesome. The best."

Maybe it was our history, maybe because we'd learned with each other, maybe other reasons I didn't want to explore right now, but tonight had been the best sex I'd had since the last time Faith and I were together.

"Then what's the problem?"

"What if she bails again?"

There it was. That was an issue for me. I knew exactly why it was an issue, and I understood in my head that it wasn't me, but I still had problems when people left me. Or ignored me.

Last year, when Faith wouldn't talk to me, I'd been devastated. It had affected my play on the ice, my classes, and I'd been a crappy roommate as well. That had all been from a misunderstanding. What if something real came between us next time? What if she just didn't love me?

"That would suck."

I nodded. He watched me, and I felt fidgety, like he was seeing things I didn't show people.

"Would it be better if she disappears in the morning, bails early?"

Would it?

"Or would it be nice to be the one bailing this time?"

I felt my mouth open as the meaning of that sank in. "I'd never do that. I lo—" I bit my tongue. I wasn't going to tell Cooper when I hadn't admitted anything to myself.

"Here's what I think, Hunter. I think none of your girlfriends have lasted because you never got over this one. So maybe, even if it goes south, you'll finally get over her. Or maybe she won't want anything to do with you after tonight, and you'll start getting over her now. But if she stays, if she wants something, you better know what you want. If you don't want anything but friends, or a hookup or whatever, then that's what you tell her. Be honest. But you get to decide what's best for you, even if it's not best for her, right?"

I stared at Cooper. He'd uncrossed his arms and was gripping the edge of the countertop. I'd never seen him this intense off the ice. He took a long breath and let it out, his hands relaxing as he shoved them in his pockets.

"Or I'm full of shit. But remember, you do what's best for you, as long as you don't make someone else pay for it." He pushed up and left the room, taking the stairs two at a time. I heard his door slam behind him.

What did I want? I sure as hell didn't want to sleep on the couch down here. It would give Faith space. She wouldn't think I was pressuring her or making assumptions. But it was too noisy here with guys coming and going, and too short for anyone over six feet. It was also lumpy. Not to mention, I didn't want the mockery that would come my way for weeks if anyone found me sleeping here.

I could wake Faith up and suggest she leave. But that would be asshole behavior. She'd just found out her grandmother only had a few weeks to live. Option three was to sleep with her. Maybe that was too girlfriendy for her, but hey, she'd fallen asleep in my bed.

She should expect that I'd sleep there, too. Shouldn't she?

11

Sebastien

Having rationalized my decision, which was what I'd wanted to do all along, I went up the stairs, drink for Faith in my hand. When I got back to my room, I opened the door quietly and peeked in. Faith hadn't moved. I set the drink by the T-shirt at her head. I took a moment to watch her softly breathing, head tucked into my pillow. I restrained myself from brushing back her hair, unsure of where we stood.

Instead, I pulled off my sweats since I never slept in them. After a pause, I grabbed my underwear and put them on. I didn't want my naked dick poking her in her sleep and making her think I was presuming things. I wasn't. I walked to the other side of the bed and slid under the covers. I lay on my back, hands behind my head, and stared at the ceiling.

Coop had given some good advice. The only problem was I didn't know what I wanted or what was best for me. For two years, that had been Faith. But now? Faith murmured in her sleep and rolled over. She snuggled into my side.

This wasn't our usual. We'd never been able to spend the night together before, always heading to our respective homes. Her parents must have had a pretty good idea what we were up to, but they hadn't given their permission, and her dad was still a pretty big guy who kept himself in shape. We'd both agreed discretion was the smarter option for us.

Last year, the weekend she was supposed to come up was going to be the first time we'd spend all night together and wake up with each other in the morning. It had never happened.

She wrapped her arm around me and moved her leg on top of mine. It felt good. So good. She was warm, her limbs heavy on me, claiming me in her sleep. Did I want to be claimed? Was I ready to risk being claimed?

I fell asleep, still without an answer.

Faith

I woke up slowly, knowing something was wrong.

It took my brain a few minutes to work things out. My head felt big, my skull tight, as if I'd been drinking. And…this didn't feel like my bed. Especially since I was wrapped around someone. I started to trace through the events of yesterday. Going to meet Seb. The phone call.

Gramma.

I stayed perfectly still, in case things might change if I didn't move, didn't accept them. But I had to breathe, and the pain hit. It was real. She was dying.

It was time to face things.

I wedged open my eyes and saw Seb's face in front of me. He was asleep, mouth relaxed, eyes closed, hair falling in his face. I'd rarely seen him asleep. And had never slept—like *slept* slept— with him. I was in bed, naked, with Seb.

The rest of the night came back. Crying all over Seb. Then coming all over him. Heat flared in my cheeks. I slowly, carefully, began to untangle our limbs.

What have I done?

This was Seb, who'd cheated…except he hadn't. My mind was

still trying to accept that completely. I didn't need to get involved with anyone, especially when I was still struggling with my classes and trying to stay on good terms with Coach. I had no idea how she'd react if I was dating one of the guys on the men's team. This was not the time to test that.

I'd moved enough that we were no longer tangled together, so I slid backward out of the sheets and ending up squatting by the bed. Naked. Naked because we'd had sex, and I'd crashed on him. I must've been so out of it last night. That was the only excuse I could come up with. I hadn't had any alcohol. I'd only overindulged in emotions.

There was a sports drink and a T-shirt on the table at the side of the bed. I blinked my eyes, realizing that Seb must have put them there. For me. That was incredibly thoughtful. Or maybe he was accustomed to this. After all, he'd dated this past year. Had been dating Holly.

Who knew how many girls he'd had here in his room? Girls he'd slept with. There could've been a lot. After all, he was a hockey player. He probably had the routine down pat. Or maybe they didn't stay over because they didn't fall asleep in his bed. He hadn't had a chance to ask me to leave. I mean, I guess he could have tried to wake me up. Maybe he had.

Now I was mortified.

I found my clothes as quietly as possible, hoping the morning light that was lifting the darkness wouldn't wake him as it helped me find my things. I pulled on my jeans, stuffing my underwear and bra in my bag. I didn't much care what I looked like to anyone outside this room, I just couldn't see Seb's face when he woke up. In case...

When I was dressed, I finally stood up, taking a quick look to make sure nothing was left behind. Then I opened the door as carefully as I used to do when I was sneaking out of my room to hook up with Seb. I drew my first normal breath when I was on the other side of his door and the latch was carefully shut. Then I fled.

I ran lightly down the stairs and grabbed my jacket and boots. I stood out on the verandah to put them on, shivering in the cold, and then I booked it. I ran like zombies were behind me. I didn't stop until I was in my own room, door locked behind me to keep those zombies out. Then I dropped to the floor. My grandmother, Seb, my own stupidity—it was a lot. I cried again, not sure what exactly I was crying about.

I was pretty sure what I'd been running from was in the room with me.

Sebastien

She was gone when I woke up.

Not really a surprise, but without even a note or text to explain, it wasn't hard to read her play. For her, last night had been a mistake. I sat, phone in hand, trying to work out my next move. Cooper had told me to decide what I wanted. I had fallen asleep trying to figure out what that was.

I woke up, thinking that the answer to that was Faith. Unfortunately, this brainstorm hit me when it looked like she wasn't feeling the same.

With Faith, I didn't have to second-guess whether she liked me because I played hockey. She did, but because that was something we had in common, not because she liked the status or possible future. If she had a choice, she wouldn't be with a hockey player. She liked me in spite of that.

She liked me, the me I'd shared with her. She *had* liked me. And she possibly was liking me as a friend again. But anything else, and she'd run.

It was the right call, obviously. Our schedules were whack, we could only hang out during the week, and I needed to decide about my future in hockey. I had classes and practices and games. It was a good time to be single. To worry only about myself. I argued really hard with myself, convincing myself I would mean it before long.

Meanwhile, I knew I should avoid Faith, because being around her would undo all the convincing I was working on so hard. Though I doubted I'd need to avoid her. Knowing Faith, she'd be avoiding me first. I still sent a text to her, just asking if she was okay. Because I wasn't an asshole. And even if she'd run, her grandmother was dying, and that was a shitty thing to have happen. She might not want me as even a friend anymore after last night, but I couldn't stop caring for her just like that.

Cooper was in the kitchen when I went down to get food before my first class. "You're alone?"

I turned in a circle. Then I shrugged. "Looks like it."

"Faith must have left early." Cooper was in running shorts and a sweatshirt, wet with perspiration.

"You were out for a run?"

He nodded. "And her boots were gone when I got up."

I was tempted, for a moment, to ask if he had a thing for boots, but it wasn't worth the effort. I knew she'd left. This information shouldn't affect me. I *knew*.

"You okay, Hunter?"

I bit back the "sure" that had popped up first, because Coop was the guy who'd helped me last year when Faith disappeared. He'd seen me at a very low place. I didn't need to try to pretend with him.

"I will be."

Cooper was leaning by the coffee machine, and he poured a cup and passed it to me.

"Maybe it's a sign, dude. Maybe it's time to join Team Fun. Find someone for today, not for the rest of eternity. You're a sophomore, for fuck's sake. Why not just have a good time for now?"

Maybe he was right. Maybe this was a sign. I had wanted what I had with Faith, but none of the other girls I'd dated had ever come close to that. I'd never wanted to be a user, a one-and-done guy, because I'd thought that was unfair to my partners. But maybe I was more of a user than I'd realized. I'd just done it over a course of weeks or months, rather than one night. Had I really committed to Holly or those girls? Or had they been placeholders? Had we broken up when they'd wanted too much from me? I hated to think that I'd used them, not been honest with them. I didn't want to be that guy.

"You might be right."

Cooper had turned to leave, but he flipped back to face me, eyes kind of bugging out. "What? Have I finally brought you over to the dark side?"

"Maybe. I don't know. Just give me a bit of time to deal with this." I was all over the place. Emotionally, this thing with Faith was messing with me. I needed some time, some thinking, and maybe a change in that thinking. It probably wasn't smart to make a decision when just hours before Faith had been wrapped in my arms.

Cooper looked like he understood. "Whatever you need, bro. But when you're ready to party, let me know."

"Thanks." I was grateful, but I wasn't there yet.

Cooper rolled his eyes. "Yeah, we'll wait until you cheer up a bit. If it's not fun, it's not worth it."

"Gotta eat before class." I opened the fridge and began to pull out the food I needed. Cooper had listened to me, advised me, and he was doing his best to understand, but he didn't, not really.

"I get it, Hunts, she's special," he said.

By the time I'd closed the fridge door to look at him, he was gone.

Faith

I had to move when Penny knocked on my door.

I would've liked to ignore her. But when she said she was worried about me and asked if I was okay, I knew I should be decent enough to tell her I was fine. I stood, drew a breath, and opened the door. She looked up at me and gasped. I must look pretty bad.

Next thing I knew, I was sitting on my bed with Penny patting my leg, saying it would be okay, and asking if I wanted tea. I hated tea.

"Tell me what he did, and we'll get him. Somehow. I know people."

I shook my head slowly. My pixie was out for blood? "Who are you planning to get?" I was still foggy, confused, and not thinking straight.

She frowned. "Sebastien must have done something. You went out to meet him yesterday, and then you didn't come back all night, and now you're like this. I thought he'd done something."

Had he? What was my problem? Seb hadn't done anything that I hadn't wanted him to do. And nothing like what Penny must be thinking if she wanted to hurt him.

I drew a breath. "My mom called. My grandmother is dying."

Penny's eyes widened, and her hand covered her mouth. "Oh, I'm so sorry, Faith! I didn't know. Is there anything I can do? Do you need to go home?"

"Gramma doesn't want me to. She wants me to keep on with hockey. Seb suggested I see if she can come down here, instead." I needed to talk to my mom. See if the doctor had okayed it.

Penny nodded. "I guess, if that's what you want. And what she wants. But since you didn't come back here... Were you with Seb last night?"

I felt the heat moving up my face, filling my cheeks. Penny's eyes grew wide. "Did you and he— Are you two?"

I dropped my face into my hands. "Yes and no. I don't know. I don't have time for this now."

Penny moved closer and wrapped her arm around me. "Hey, if that got you through a bad night, that's great. But what did you guys decide going forward?"

I shook my head. I could hear the frown in her voice.

"Faith, what happened? Didn't you guys talk?"

I was confused and upset, and this wasn't something I could talk about with my mom or my teammates, but maybe I could with Penny. "We talked about my grandmother, and then I cried all over him, and somehow, I don't know, we kissed, and then, yeah, sex. I fell asleep, like, before I could even get dressed, and when I woke up...I just left."

"Faith." Penny sounded serious, so I lifted my head.

"You two didn't plan to have sex, and you did, and you didn't talk about it?"

I shook my head, slowly, then nodded. I was so confused.

"Not at all?"

I shook my head again.

"How are you feeling?"

I let out a long breath. "Mixed up. I'm sad about my grand-mother, and mad at Seb, and I kind of want to punch myself..."

"Okay." Penny nodded. "Let's go through this. Sad about grandmother, understood. But why are you mad at Seb?"

"Because—" I stopped. In my head, I still hadn't rewritten last year. I'd been angry, sad, disappointed for most of the year because he'd cheated. But that wasn't what had really happened, and I was still adjusting. I needed to change that, because it wasn't fair to him.

"You get what the problem is with that, right?"

I nodded.

"I guess you still need time to process that one. Now, why do you want to punch yourself?"

"Because I don't want to get involved with anyone. Sleeping with Seb was stupid. I'm finally doing better with Coach and classes, and I don't have time to date anyone."

She blinked at me. "Does that mean you want to date Seb?"

Penny was too good at this. Did I want to? Did I want to even think about this now?

"I don't know. I mean, we were good together before he came here."

"And—" Penny lowered her voice, "—the sex?"

My cheeks heated up again. "Good. Um, really good."

Now I could say that because I had something to compare it to. Like I'd told Cooper, I'd rebounded. I'd refused to let a cheater be my last sex partner. I'd been suspicious of almost any guy back then, but when I was finally ready, I'd gone to a doctor to see what to do about the condom issue and found out about non-latex options.

That had been the easy part. Finding a guy had been more of a problem. I didn't want a boyfriend, and I didn't want to hook up with someone local. Finally, at a tournament, I'd met a guy. He'd been interested, and we'd gone to his room. It had been fine, and after, I'd been able to say I'd rebounded. But in a way, I hadn't. Because just-fine sex wasn't really getting over Seb.

I'd met someone else at hockey camp over the summer, and he'd been nice. We got along, and he was attracted enough to me to actually pursue me. We'd hooked up, and it had been better than fine. He'd wanted something more, to be boyfriend and girlfriend. Although I'd still been hating on Seb then, I hadn't been able to stop comparing how it had been with Seb and I, and how it was with him. It wasn't as good. And I wasn't going to settle for second best.

I was single. I'd planned to stay that way.

Penny was watching me with narrowed eyes. "Was Seb your first?"

I nodded.

"And have you been with anyone else?"

I nodded again.

"So how does Seb rank compared to anyone else?"

I closed my eyes, more embarrassed than I should be about discussing this. "He's the best. Still."

Penny's hand was stroking mine, like I was a cat she was calming. "Well, maybe you could do friends with benefits with him? If you don't want to date, maybe it's a way to get the best of both worlds.

Could I?

Maybe I could have done that with some guys. But I had real doubts that I could be friends the way we used to and sleep with him like we used to do without running into feelings like we used to have. I didn't think I was up to that. I was still torn between Seb, the guy I'd loved, and the cheater I'd hated, because they'd been tangled together for so long. Now I was mixing in Seb, my current friend, and I had to sift through the real parts of my memories and the mistaken parts.

"I don't know."

"And what about him?"

What did Seb want? He'd never made a move, never indicated he wanted more than friendship. And I'd seen his exes. Penny's talk about IG had led me to search through Seb's and the men's hockey team's accounts. I'd seen photos of him with three different girls, all at different times. Three petite, brunette, thin, and pretty girls. Penny was closer to Seb's type than I was.

It hit me then. I'd started things last night. Not Seb. I'd gone to kiss his cheek. I'm the one who'd dug up the condoms. Not Seb. I had instigated everything. It had been a pity fuck. Seb wasn't looking to start things up again. We were friends, and he'd felt bad for me. Just like he'd felt bad for me when he'd helped with Coach and with my psych class.

"No, Penny, he doesn't want anything like that. It was just one of those things, you know? Thanks for helping me work this out."

And now that I had worked it out, I should answer Seb's text. I should send something like *Sure, I'm fine*, or *I'll get through it*, or something. We were— We'd been friends. It was weird that I was making it weird by not responding. But I didn't want him to explain to me that sleeping together hadn't meant anything. I was fragile, and that wasn't something I felt like I could cope with right now. Not responding was my way to let him know I got it.

When a couple of days went by, and he didn't call or text, I knew we understood each other.

12

Sebastien

I didn't have good practices that week. It wasn't hard to figure out why.

I understood Faith didn't want us to start up again, but I was twisted up inside that she'd ghosted me *again*. She didn't respond to my text, didn't reach out, and I hadn't seen her at all.

It didn't matter what I wanted when she didn't want anything. But it would have been nice to talk like adults. I'd made sure all along the way that night that she was with me. She'd agreed. She'd fucking consented. She could at least answer my text. It made me angry, and that was good. Because otherwise, I might have been upset. I might have been hurt. And I wasn't doing that again. I was tired and distracted, and I could tell Coach noticed, but he didn't say anything.

Instead, Cooper barged into my room. "Get any bad news from your family?"

I looked up from the textbook I'd been staring at but not actually reading. I frowned at him. "No, not that I know of."

"Classes going okay?"

If I could stop my mind from spinning on a hamster wheel over Faith, classes would be fine. "Yes."

"So it's Faith." He frowned at me.

"What's Faith?" I knew what he meant, but I was going to make him say it. It was petty, and I didn't care.

He sighed, like I was a three-year-old giving him a hard time. Perhaps that wasn't a bad comparison, because I'd enjoy a temper tantrum right now. Screaming and throwing things.

"That's why you're moping. Did she tell you no more hooking up? Only friends?"

Cooper was almost more invested in this non-relationship than I was. But it was my life, not his. "No." I hoped he'd leave if I didn't start talking.

"She doesn't even want to be friends anymore? That's harsh. Or you really need some coaching on pleasing your partners, Hunts."

I felt my fists clenching. I looked up at my ceiling. It wasn't much to look at. "I know how to please my partner, asshole. That wasn't the problem." I knew Faith had come and come hard. I knew her body and how it responded as well as I knew my own. She could complain about a lot of things, but not that she hadn't enjoyed the sex that night. We both had.

Cooper rested his hands on his hips. "You mean, she wanted to be with you again and *you* said no?"

That wasn't a possibility, because it would involve Faith actually talking to me. "No, Cooper, she didn't say that, either. She didn't say anything."

He cocked his head. I could see him out of the corner of my eye.

"Did you reach out to her?"

"Of course, I did. I sent her a text and asked how she was. She didn't respond."

Just like last time. But this time, I wasn't frantically reaching out every way I could to try to speak to her. I'd done that once. Doing it now would be desperation on a different scale. There was no misunderstanding to clear up. Faith had disappeared on me. Again.

"Did you call her? Go see her?"

I pushed myself up, letting the book close. "What's the point, Coop? She didn't even answer the text. She doesn't want anything to do with me. I'm not going to push myself on her. Once was enough."

Cooper didn't understand any of this because he wasn't the one texting after hooking up. He didn't do that, as far as I could tell. He was the one avoiding texts or calls or any repeats. Why the hell he thought he could help with my problems, I didn't know.

Okay, he'd helped before. But I'd be happy if he'd just butt out now.

"What if the text didn't go through, or it somehow got erased before she read it? What if she replied, and her answer didn't go through to you?"

I could feel my jaw drop, and I must have looked like an idiot. "I didn't think of that."

I wasn't sure what to do. If Faith had decided to cut off communication, then I didn't want to be the desperate guy following her around, stalking her and begging her to reconsider. But what if she hadn't gotten the message? What if she'd answered and thought I was ghosting *her*?

Cooper glared at me. "Honestly, the two of you are worse than Romeo and Juliet. If there was any poison around here, you'd both be dead."

What was it with Cooper and *Romeo and Juliet*?

"How do I find out what's happened? Should I go over there?" Now I wanted his advice. If there was a chance that Faith wasn't repeating what happened last year…

"What are you going to say to her?"

I shrugged. I hadn't even thought of this thirty seconds ago. It wasn't like I had an essay written out to guide me. "I don't know."

"Then maybe you'd better not head over just yet or we *will* have someone putting a dagger in their chest. The way you two make getting together as difficult as possible, it's going to happen yet. Tell you what, the girls' hockey house has a party tomorrow night. Faith should be there. I'll talk to her, try to figure things out. You be there in case there's a chance for you, and try not to look like a sad sack, 'cause that's not going to help anyone."

On the one hand, the smart move was probably to be direct and for me to talk to Faith and not use Cooper as an intermediary. On the other hand, I had no idea what to say. What if she had gotten my text? Then I'd be embarrassed and feel totally stupid, like I didn't understand what not responding was supposed to tell me. If she didn't get it, should I apologize for not following up?

And on the other hand, if I was allowed three, Cooper had done pretty well so far. He was right. Faith and I did have a history of making things difficult. That was something we needed to fix *if* she wasn't trying to make me disappear from her life.

Cooper might not be interested in a relationship with a girl, but he was doing pretty well helping me. I'd have to ask him about that sometime. But I wasn't going to risk pissing him off right now.

"Sure," I agreed, and he left the room muttering under his breath.

Cooper had told me to make sure I knew what I wanted with Faith. Not hearing from her for most of a week had clarified it. I wanted to be friends with her, at the very least. And if we could be more, be together? I wanted that. More than was probably good for me.

I had second thoughts while getting ready for the party. More like thirtieth or fortieth thoughts. I'd been wavering back and forth ever since I talked to Cooper. I'm not sure why I was placing so much trust in him. It wasn't like he'd ever been in any kind of relationship as far as I knew, certainly not since he'd been at Moo U. Instead, he'd been single-minded about *not* being tied to anyone.

Cooper had gotten Faith to listen to him about what had happened last year, which was more than I'd been able to do.

Holding on to that thought, I did what he told me to do. I made sure I looked nice for the party, and once I got there, I didn't immediately try to find her. I wanted to, but I was also worried about what she might do if she saw me. She might ignore me or refuse to look at me, and I was pretty sure I couldn't handle that.

The parties at the women's hockey house were a little different than ours. They tended to have a more equal balance of the sexes, and more on offer than kegs and chips. I'll admit we were pretty lazy in our party planning.

My gaze started to roam the room, and I reminded myself I wasn't supposed to look for Faith, so I shouldn't look for my teammates, either, in case she was talking to them. That didn't leave me with many options. I hoped Cooper would do whatever he was going to do quickly. Maybe I should just grab a drink and hide in a corner until I found out what Faith had said to him.

I made my way to the kitchen and got some beer, but there was a kind of mixed drink there as well—vodka and some juice. Not like it was a huge effort, but it was more than we ever did. I grabbed a handful of chips, because even though I appreciated that they had more variety of snacks available, I liked the boring stuff. With my cup of beer, I headed into the next room, which had some new faces. Mostly women, but no one I'd met before. There were no tall blondes, so I was safe in this room for now.

I wasn't one of the most noticeable guys on the team, but I had been playing well this season, and I guess people were starting to recognize me. The girls in this room did, at least. I found myself the filling in a pretty girl sandwich, if five women and me could be called that? I could tell they were impressed I was on the hockey team, and that wasn't something I liked, not in a girl-friend. But since Faith had disappeared after we'd had sex, and then hadn't reached out to me, my ego enjoyed the confidence boost. It was hard to stay in a bad mood when attractive women were acting like you'd made their night. They were focused on me and it seemed like everything I said was interesting.

With the beer and the attention, my mood began to change. I

wasn't a troll. If Faith didn't want anything between us, that didn't mean I was going to end up alone, or drink poison, or whatever other gloomy scenario Cooper was dreaming of.

I didn't like that Cooper was getting into my head. I answered questions about what it was like to play hockey and to explain icing, which I swear was posted somewhere online as a question to ask guys who played hockey, because everyone asked me that. I enjoyed the attention, because damn it, this was a party, and I deserved to have a bit of fun. Of course, that was as far as it went. I was still hung up on Faith, so I wasn't going to be an asshole and use anyone to make me feel less of a loser.

I didn't ask any of them out or respond to the veiled offers I got. If I'd wanted, I could have gone to someone's dorm room— not to study—or had my dick sucked in the bathroom. Not the first time I'd had offers. I had pretty well reached my limit and was about to excuse myself to go get some more beer and look for a teammate or some reason to escape when I felt a finger loop into my belt loop and tug.

I turned to ask what the hell, because *come on*, but once I saw who the finger belonged to, I froze. I could do nothing but stare as the sounds of the party faded away.

Faith

I didn't want to go to the party. I knew there was a good chance Seb would be there, and I didn't want to see him. I'd been acting like a baby by refusing to answer that text. I knew that, and yet I still hadn't answered. And the longer I didn't answer, the harder it got. I wanted to pretend nothing had happened. To take that night, as great as it had been, and put it in that Seb box I had and lock it away. Except there wasn't much left in that box. The horrible things from last year, the ones I'd been so hurt by, didn't really exist. There were just a few things that I'd tried to ignore from this year left in there. The almost kiss at the rink the first day

I saw him. Some weird reactions I had to seeing him and being with him. And that night.

I knew I was behaving badly. We'd been friends these past few weeks, best friends, at least for me. I'd hadn't gotten that close to anyone on my team, and Penny, great as she was, couldn't be that. Her interests were different, and we didn't have history, not like Seb and I did.

Cutting Seb out like this because I was afraid to find out he thought it was a mistake meant I didn't have my friend, either. He'd been so great, comforting me, letting me cry all over him, and his idea about having Gramma come to a game was golden. I'd talked to Coach, and due to the special circumstances, she'd agreed to pencil me in as starter, assuming I didn't break a limb or start sucking on the ice. I was determined not to. I was going to have my grandmother watch me one more time…

I had to swallow and blink fast. Shouldn't I be handling her illness better by now? I'd had almost a week to come to terms with it, but it still hurt to think about. If only things had ended when he'd come up with that idea. If only I hadn't kissed him and then climbed him. I'm sure he hadn't hated it. I mean, it was sex, and I thought it was good. He'd certainly acted like it was great. But we were done, and I shouldn't have crossed that line.

He'd kept asking if I wanted it. If *I* wanted it. I'd never asked if he did. Maybe he wouldn't have told me the truth even if I'd asked him. He'd felt sorry for me, and maybe sex was something he'd done to make me feel better, to forget. I should've talked to him. But the thought of hearing him say it was a mistake, that we shouldn't do it again, or that I shouldn't think we were something other than friends made my skin crawl.

I had two good reasons to skip the party. I wanted to avoid Seb and I wasn't in a party mood because of my grandmother. But there was one good reason to go. The party was for Anderson, our starting goalie's birthday. Things were improving with Coach and the team and staying away from something specifically planned for the woman I wanted to replace would not look good.

Coach had done me a favor by almost guaranteeing me a start. But if I then acted like I wasn't part of the team; she might think I was pulling something, manipulating her. Maybe I was wrong, but I was still worried she believed I didn't want to play on her team. I had to at least make an appearance, wish Anders a happy birthday, and then I could make my excuses. With any luck, I could avoid Seb. It wasn't for sure that he'd be there. But I'd thought that before and been wrong.

Penny was coming with me for moral support. She wasn't with her basketball guy any longer, so maybe she had other motives, but I was grateful. I'd bought some more skirts and tops that she'd approved for the parties I was coming to realize were frequent. Most of my teammates went with what I'd called a girlie look. I was more comfortable with it now, and since I didn't feel like Frankenstein around the other women on my team, I kind of liked dressing up a bit.

College was already broadening my horizons. Go me!

We arrived a little late, since I wanted a crowd there when we arrived to make sure I could avoid Seb. It was stupid, but there was a lot going on in my head with my grandmother, school, and hockey, and I just didn't need anything else to make me sad. Of course, not talking to him was making me feel anxious and nervous and stressed, but I'd never claimed to be a genius.

There was a good crowd, and the music was loud. We made it inside and I saw the first room was Seb free. I decided to stay in the Seb-free zone and asked Penny if she would get me a drink. I'd figure out where my teammate was so I could wish her happy birthday and then I could leave.

I lost sight of Penny almost immediately, her copper hair quickly disappearing amongst the taller crowd. I did see a couple of my teammates and stopped to talk with them. They had a beer for me, and I took it since I had a strong suspicion Penny had been sidetracked and wasn't coming back. I'd started to relax when I felt a tug on my hair.

I knew it was Seb. Time to face the music. I whipped around, ready with an apology. But it wasn't Seb. It was Cooper. I wasn't sure if it was relief or disappointment I felt, but it was something that made my stomach tense.

He leaned toward my ear. "We need to talk, Juliet."

I examined his face, not sure he was drunk enough this early to confuse me with someone else, someone called Juliet. He appeared sober and jerked his head.

"Give me a sec," I told my teammates and then followed Cooper, wondering if Seb had asked him to talk to me. If he somehow thought I was this Juliet, I'd give him a hard time for mixing us up.

There were people on the veranda, but he led the way to a quiet corner. No one was close. It was cold enough that fewer people were hanging out on the porches than earlier in the season. Cooper leaned against the wall and narrowed his eyes. He looked way too much like Prof Warner had those first few weeks. I didn't know what he wanted to talk about, but I knew I was getting a D. I had a suspicion the subject of our conversation was going to be Seb. I braced myself.

"Did you get a text from Seb after you spent the night with him? And if you did, did you answer?"

The beer I'd drunk suddenly wanted to make a reappearance. "Uh, what business is it of yours, and why are you asking?"

Was it Seb? Had he asked Cooper to talk to me? If Seb didn't want to talk in person, things must be bad. Being cut off from Seb again would be painful. Him regretting that night would hurt. A lot. But isn't that what I was doing, making that happen by ignoring him?

"Hunter is my partner on the ice, and when he's moping, he plays like shit. So we're not passing notes like we're back in high school, and playing I thought he or she was doing what the hell ever. Did you get his text?"

This was the Cooper who'd made me face up to what Seb hadn't done last year. I answered with a nod.

"Did you answer him?"

This time I gave a shake of my head.

"Why the fuck not?"

I opened my mouth to explain, and nothing came out. How was I supposed to explain myself when I was still a knot of confusion and nervousness?

"Faith, it's not fair to play games with him. I expected better of you."

Cooper being disappointed with me hadn't been on my bingo card, but he was right. I pulled on my hair, trying to find a way to explain this. I wasn't sure I understood it all myself.

"He told you about my grandmother?" Cooper knew so much, he must know that, but I wanted to be sure.

"Yes, and I'm sorry about that."

I swallowed. "Thanks. It's...not been easy trying to accept that. And Seb was so nice... I just don't think I'm ready for him to tell me it didn't mean anything."

Cooper frowned. "What didn't mean anything? Sex?"

My cheeks heated. Obviously, Cooper must know what happened. The house they lived in wasn't big enough for overnight guests to be a secret. But I wasn't used to speaking so bluntly. I must seem incredibly stupid or manipulative for not answering Seb's text, so I had to try to defend myself.

"I've seen the girls he's gone out with since we broke up. I'm not his type, not anymore, and I get that. But I just... I don't know. I just can't deal with him letting me down easy right now."

Cooper looked more like Prof Warner than ever. "First of all, ignoring it doesn't make it go away, and it doesn't help anyone. It's hurting Seb. You're ghosting him again, and he doesn't deserve it this time, either."

I flinched.

"And secondly, those girls he's dated? They've been his anti-type. He might not have figured this out himself, but he's always avoided anyone like you."

I searched Cooper's face, trying to understand what he was saying. Isn't that what I just said?

"Why would he do that?" I mean, other than the obvious conclusion that he *liked* pretty, petite brunettes.

"Come on, Faith, you're smarter than that."

Did that mean something, that he went out with girls who were not like me? And what could it mean?

"He doesn't regret that night? I mean, I cried all over him first, and then I fell asleep in his bed after. He didn't even get a chance to ask me to leave."

Cooper snorted. "Right, like he would've."

"Cooper, please, just tell me, 'cause I don't know what I'm doing. Does he want more? Like what we had before?"

"Do you?"

I guess that was fair. Before sharing what was going on with Seb, he wanted to know about me. I'd been wavering, but mostly, I'd been afraid. Afraid that my insecurities from a year ago, the hang-ups I had, the way I'd blocked him, had all been too much. Enough that he didn't want to try again. I mean, it's not like he'd made a move on me since I'd been here. Sure, he'd been willing to be friends again, but now?

He was part of the popular men's hockey team. He'd been dating other girls. Hadn't he realized he could do better than me? But would Cooper be here talking to me if that were the case? It suddenly hit hard how much I wanted what we'd had before.

I nodded. "Yeah, think I do."

Cooper grabbed my arm and dragged me to a window. He stood behind me and used his hands to position my head so that I had to look where he wanted. My stomach tightened up again, and my heartbeat stuttered. Seb was in the back room. Seeing him made my pulse accelerate and nerves twist up my stomach, as if I were starting an important game. My body knew what I wanted, even if my mind was running in circles. But Seb was with a bunch of girls. Pretty, admiring girls who wouldn't flake out on him.

I swallowed. "He looks...busy." I worked hard to make sure my voice didn't betray me.

Cooper snorted. "You lift a finger. One finger. And he's yours."

I stood for a moment. Considered what Cooper had said. On the ice, I was brave. Never flinched from a shot, coming out of my crease to challenge a shooter, willing to take chances. This was different. But maybe I could call up some of that courage. Maybe I needed to know. Getting an answer I didn't want would hurt, but I could deal with it and move on.

I turned to face Cooper. "Okay, I'll lift a finger and see what happens."

I honestly expected him to laugh at me. He didn't.

"Finally. My job is done. I believe there's someone in there waiting for me, so I'll trust you two are good now."

"Who?" I was curious about Cooper's plans. I mean, he'd stuck his nose well into my business.

He shrugged. "Don't know yet."

Uggh. Give me Seb any day. Speaking of which, I made my way back into the house. I wove around bodies with one destination in mind. I could see Seb ahead of me, my height an advantage. He hadn't seen me yet. I came up behind him, took a finger like Cooper had suggested, slid it into his belt loop, and tugged.

I held my breath, afraid of what might happen.

He turned, looking annoyed. Then he looked surprised. Not pissed. Definitely not pissed. That sparked more courage. I used my other hand to grip the back of his head, and I kissed him.

13

Sebastien

Seeing Faith behind me was a shock. Especially since the look on her face was... And then she kissed me. I'd been upset with her, wanted to ask why she'd blown me off, if she had. Why she'd run after that night together. What she wanted. But none of that mattered, not here, not now, not while she was kissing me.

I wrapped one arm around her waist and threaded my other hand through her hair, holding her to me. I was almost afraid she'd vanish again. But she ran her tongue along the seam of my lips, and I opened to her, and then I wasn't afraid. I wasn't thinking, just pouring myself into the kiss.

She tasted like beer and hope and Faith, and I never wanted to stop. I pulled away when I got dizzy and realized it was from lack of oxygen, not a surfeit of Faith. At least, I thought it was.

We were touching, chest to knees. My skin prickled, goosebumps rising, legs feeling weak. Slowly, the sounds of the party around me came back, but all I could see was Faith, her expression open and warm. Her face was right there, no need to kink my neck or bend my knees. Right there, at the perfect height for us to kiss for days, just as long as I remembered to breathe.

We should try that sometime.

"Hey." I had a lot of other things I wanted to say, things like *Does this mean we're back together?* And *Why didn't you get back to me?* But I didn't want to say any of that right now. I wasn't sure I wanted those answers at the moment. I just wanted this, more of it, as often as I could have it.

"Hey." She was a little breathless, and I probably was, too. Didn't care.

"Um." She bit her lip. "I need to say happy birthday to Anders, and see what Penny's doing. Then maybe we should get out of here?"

I nodded. I just hoped we were getting out of here to do more of the kissing kind of stuff.

I slipped her hand in mine, prepared to take any advantage I could. She flashed a grin at me and led me through the house.

I'd follow her anywhere.

When we got to the birthday girl, Coop was there. He looked at me, then at our hands linked together, and he smirked. I didn't know what exactly he'd done, but I was grateful.

Thanks I mouthed, and then I followed Faith again as we tracked down her roommate.

Penny's eyebrows shot up when she saw us, and then she smiled, big and wide. It was a good night for smiling. She told Faith she was good to get home on her own, and then we were free to grab our coats and leave. We had to separate while we put on our coats and gloves, but once we were walking out the door, I reached for Faith's hand again and found hers seeking mine. I gripped her gloved fingers tightly and let her lead the way.

She led us back to her dorm. Good idea, since I think some of my roommates were still at the hockey house, and I didn't want to talk to anyone right now. We walked in silence. I didn't know what Faith was thinking. I wasn't thinking much of anything. For the moment, I was happy just to enjoy this.

Once we made it to her room and shut the door, I turned and pushed her against the wall. I framed her face in my hands and pressed my lips to hers. She opened, and there was that connection again. A connection I'd only found with her.

I could feel my dick waking up, ready to take this further, but I didn't press against her. I didn't want to risk spooking her. I would take sex off the table if we could be together and keep kissing.

I wanted lots and lots of kissing. Like when we first were together, before either of us took that next step. Faith melted into me for minutes or hours and then pushed me away.

"No, we need to talk, Seb." Her voice was ragged.

I sighed, dragging in air. Her lips were swollen from our kisses, and her pupils were large in those amazing eyes. Her hair was mussed, and her skin was flushed.

Mine was, too, I was sure.

I wanted to keep kissing her. I was afraid talking was going to end this.

"I know, but one more—"

"No!" She slipped out of my reach. "One more kiss, and we'll be naked in bed."

I jerked forward, toward her, unable to stop myself. Was she trying to kill me?

She held up a hand. "I'd rather do that, but I think it'll be better if we talk first."

That depended on how the talk went, but she was right. I knew she was right, but I'd never wanted to do the wrong thing more. "Okay."

Faith pulled off her coat, and I did the same with mine. Then she pulled out a desk chair for me. She set it down at the far side of her room and pointed for me to sit in it while she sat down on the bed.

I sat, unsure what to do with my arms, or legs, or anything really. I was cautiously optimistic after that kiss, but I wasn't sure what Faith wanted. At least there was no more doubt about what I wanted.

I wanted her.

"First, I apologize for not answering your text."

She had ghosted me. There hadn't been any problem with her phone like Cooper had suggested. That made my stomach clench and my mind focus on something other than touching Faith. I wanted some answers.

"Why didn't you?"

Her gaze skittered away from me. "Because I was afraid it was a pity fuck."

It took time for those words to sink in. They didn't make sense. And when they did, I was angry. "What the hell, Faith?"

"I'm sorry, Seb, but I'd been crying, and I was a mess, and I've seen the girls you've dated. I thought… Well, I didn't feel confident. You kept asking if I was sure, but I didn't ask you. I thought maybe you were just horny or felt like you wanted to comfort me or… I dunno. My mind was scrambled. And I thought I was over you, so it shouldn't bother me, but—"

I latched on to the words that grabbed my attention. "You *thought* you were over me?"

She was twisting strands of her hair around her finger, watching the ends of her fingers turning red, not meeting my gaze.

"I was so angry at you, and so hurt—"

"But, Faith, I swear, I never—"

"I *know* Seb, I get it. I do. But for a whole year, I thought you *had*, and it took a while to get past that. Sometimes I still forget. And after we…hooked up—"

"It wasn't a hookup, Faith." I knew I sounded intense. I felt intense. I needed her to know that I didn't do hookups, and that I especially didn't do them with her.

She looked at me, brow creased, teeth pulling on her lip. "No?"

I shook my head. "That's not me."

She sighed. "I'm sorry, but that's where my head was at. I was worried about my grandmother and was kind of messed up."

Fuck. I should have thought of that. If I hadn't been focused on me, and my being butt-hurt, I might have considered what she was going through.

"I wasn't sure what you wanted, and I didn't know what I wanted, and I was really confused."

I just wished she'd felt like she could talk to me. Damn it, I should have tried to reach out again. Fuck my stupid pride.

"I'm sorry, Faith. I should've realized you had a lot going on. I didn't need to make it worse. Have you made up your mind?"

I thought she must have. She'd come to the party and kissed me. We were here, talking. And she'd said she'd *thought* she'd gotten over me, and that sounded to me like she hadn't, not really.

"Cooper." She rested her head in her hands. "I cannot believe I'm taking advice from Cooper, of all people."

I grinned. "I know. Same here. But he's a good friend, even if he's not really someone who does relationships."

She eyed me suspiciously. "What did he tell you?"

"That I need to figure out what I want and then talk to you. I went to the party looking for you." Well, that was why I'd been there, though I hadn't technically looked for her. I'd trusted Cooper and waited to get a signal from him. Then Faith had come up and…that must have been the signal. I owed Cooper.

"I found you first." Faith's expression… Was it getting flirty?

"Cooper told me not to talk to you until he did."

Faith flopped back on her bed. "Oh my God. He totally did get us together."

I looked at Faith. I could read between the lines, but I was desperate to get a clear answer from her. "Did he? Are we together?"

Her eyes were round. "Do you want to be?"

I was committing here. If she didn't feel the same… "Absolutely. You?"

"I think so."

And there was the punch to the gut. But think so was miles

better than where we'd been last year or at the beginning of the school year.

"You think so? How do I convince you?"

Faith pushed herself back so that she was stretched out on her bed. She traced her lip with her tongue. "Kissing would be a good start."

I stood up from the chair and walked the two steps to her bed. I put a knee on it and leaned down, one hand resting beside her. I looked at her face, searched her eyes.

"Are you sure, Faith? No joking, for real." I needed to know she was all in. Last year, losing her had been devastating, but at least I hadn't had to watch her on campus, see her avoid me, see her rebound with someone else. The thought of having to do that caused a physical pain.

She looked up at me with a serious expression. She knew my flaws, the issues I had thanks to my family. She *knew* me. Me, Seb, ordinary guy, not Hunter, the defenseman for the hockey team.

She reached up a hand, cupped it over my cheek. "Absolutely."

I closed my eyes and leaned into her hand. I wanted to kiss her. To ignite that fire that kissing her always ignited in me. In us. But she'd agreed we were back together. I didn't know how she imagined we'd do that. It's not like I thought she'd want to have a chaste, celibate relationship, but I didn't want to push. We'd been friends, gotten back to that, and then sex had made her run.

I'd suffer blue balls as long as necessary to make sure we got it right this time.

I opened my eyes and drew back enough to lie down beside her. I braced my head on my hand so I could watch her expression, read her body language.

"How do you want to do this?"

Her brows met in a frown. "What do you mean?"

"Do you want to pull back a bit, keep it to kissing, or what?"

Her eyes went wide, and she pushed herself up. She swung a leg over me, so she was sitting on me, shoving me flat onto my back. "I'm not pulling back anything. We've got some lost time to make up for."

My dick twitched, liking the sound of that. And then Faith leaned down, her hands on my chest, and kissed me.

Faith

Okay, it was kind of sweet that Seb was willing to take it slow if I wanted to. But I'd finally made my decision. I wasn't wasting any more time. I bent down to kiss him, enjoying the moan he made when our lips made contact. In this position, I could feel he was getting hard beneath me, so his body was fully on board.

It gave me confidence.

I nipped his lip, teasing his mouth open while my hands reached down to his waist and slipped up under his sweater. I felt him shiver as I traced my fingers up his ribs, brushing over his pecs, teasing his nipples, and dragging his clothing up with my hands.

When I'd managed to push the sweater up to his arms, he used his hands on my waist to push me back up. Then he sat up, those abs he worked on for hockey lifting him effortlessly, letting me pull his clothing up over his head.

I was ready to reward his hard work with my hands and my mouth.

I tried to flatten my hands over his chest, but he was on board now and taking an active role. He tugged on my top, and as I raised my arms, he whipped it over my head. He dropped back on the bed, gaze hot on my chest. I was burning up, scorched by his gaze. I reached back, undid my bra, and pulled it off to drop it on the floor. His hands gently stroked my body, and I closed my eyes, enjoying the soft touch.

"Gorgeous." He breathed the words, and I felt gorgeous. He'd always made me feel more attractive than I knew myself to be. He tugged me down again, bringing my breasts to his mouth, where he gently kissed the peaks.

I could feel that touch raising goosebumps over my skin that travelled over my body and pooled heat between my legs. I was ready to move on from sweet and gentle. I ran my hands into his hair, tugging, my hips grinding down on the erection I could feel under me. I was on fire, desperate for more contact, more everything.

He circled my nipple with his tongue and then closed his lips and tugged. I gasped, desperate to both bring him closer and to shove him away to get rid of the last of our clothes. The two choices conflicted, and my brain wasn't able to make a decision.

Another rub on his groin, and he shuddered.

"Pants. Off." I gasped.

With a last swirl of his tongue, he pulled away. His cheeks were flushed, his eyes half closed. This was a Seb I knew. We'd taught each other this dance, step by step, and I knew his body and how he reacted. I knew he closed his eyes when I touched his cock, his brow creasing as if he was in pain. I knew if I ran my tongue over his balls, his hips would shoot up, almost hitting me in the face. I knew how he tasted.

I wanted to reacquaint myself with everything.

I pushed on Seb, and he twisted, and we conked heads as we struggled to get the rest of our clothes off. I had my hands on his zipper, and he slapped them away. I flopped back and then shoved my pants down my legs with shaking hands while he kicked his jeans and boxer briefs off his feet. His erection jutted out, just like I remembered. I stopped, panting and watching him.

Last time, when I'd been crying and upset, I hadn't taken the appropriate amount of time to watch, to appreciate how he'd changed over the last year. It deserved to be savored. His muscles were bigger, more defined. There was more hair on his chest and trailing down to his groin. I was sure his frame was bigger, his stubble thicker than it had been. He stopped, watching me watch him. We paused for a moment, staring at each other's naked bodies, and for me, it was a chance to absorb what was happening.

Me. Seb. Together again.

It felt right. Necessary.

Inevitable.

Sebastien

Faith was staring at me, at my body, her gaze admiring, and every crunch, every weight, every run was worth it to see that look in her eyes. Then she lifted that gaze to my face, and I knew she saw me, not just my body. Unlike the other girls I'd been with, Faith saw me and knew me and wanted to be with me. It made what we did together so much better.

Her pants were around her knees. I didn't know why she'd stopped, but I was happy to take whatever time she needed so I could just feast on her body. Okay, my dick was impatient, but we both admired the view.

Faith worked as hard as I did to keep herself in shape. She was strong, and her muscles were moulded and defined, light and shadow. She doubted how feminine they were, but I thought they were beautiful. Her nipples were hard and still wet from my mouth. Her chest was rising and falling, as if she'd just played a hard game, but it was from me. For me.

For us.

Suddenly, she snapped back. "Condoms, top drawer."

She reached to take off what was left of her clothing, and I turned over to follow her directions. I pulled out the drawer and grasped for the familiar foil packs. I grabbed a couple, feeling optimistic about more than one chance, and suddenly, she was pressed against me.

Naked skin to naked skin. Her boobs against my back. She snuck her arm around my waist, and her hand travelled down, brushing over my abs and hip.

"I want to spend some time with that—" She brushed her fingers against my erection, and I almost levitated off the bed. "But after. Right now, we need that condom, fast."

I almost laughed, but I was too desperate to be inside her. I ripped the package open with trembling fingers. I pulled it out and rolled it on with real urgency. Faith drew away, and when I moved back to face her, I found her lying on her back.

"Like this." She stretched her arms over her head. "I want to see your face."

I pushed up on my arms, but before moving on her, I leaned in to kiss her, slow and sweet, wanting to make sure she knew this was real. It wasn't pity. It was more than sex. I was all in.

She shivered. "Now, Seb."

I kneeled between her legs, taking in the new angle. Her aroused body was spread out for me. I looked down at her pussy. Her curls were wet and waiting. I wanted to thank her for giving me another chance. To let her know I'd never hurt her. But she was impatient, gripping my hips and pulling me down for another kiss.

And then I was inside her again, and it was everything. Her wet heat, her moans, her hands digging into my skin, pulling me closer, her strong legs wrapped around my waist, her hips, rising to meet me. I pulled back, almost all the way out, and then plunged back in, and she moved to meet me. I rested on my arms, framing her body, and her eyes locked on mine.

"Seb," she whispered, and it was us again. I moved, watching every response on her face, feeling every clench of her pussy on me, and when she became frantic, I moved my fingers to her clit, pressing and watching her fall apart around me, her inner walls pulling on me.

It was more than I could take. I shuddered and felt my own orgasm barrel through me, and I was lost, nothing but Faith in my consciousness.

Faith

Seb was heavy on me, but I didn't care. The aftershocks were still working through my body, and I lay with my eyes closed, focusing on simply breathing in and out. I wanted to feel like this always.

Seb drew in a long breath and exhaled against my neck, tickling me and making me squirm. He braced himself back up on his arms and withdrew. My body was reluctant to let him go, and he flopped down on the bed beside me. He reached out, his hand searching for mine, and he turned his head. I saw his expression change, concern creasing his forehead. I pushed my face forward and traced a gentle kiss on his lips. The frown vanished, a smile chasing it away.

"You're good?" His voice was still raspy. When I ran a finger down his chest, he shivered.

"Very good. You?"

"Incredible."

I smiled, a smug smile. But damn it, that *had* been incredible, and I'd been part of it. Team effort.

Seb squeezed my hand. "Be back in a moment." He grabbed the condom and left for the en suite bathroom.

Not gonna lie, I watched that tight ass walk away and kept smiling. Because that was mine now. Right? Maybe I should clarify just what we were now.

I pushed myself up, so I missed some of the Seb show as he walked back in. There must have been something on my face, because he paused for a fraction of a second, and the worried look returned to his face.

"What is it, Faith?"

I didn't want to worry him. I just wanted to know where we stood before I invested too much of myself. Though I wasn't sure I could pull back without a lot of hurt.

"What are we exactly? We talked about being back together, but what does that mean?"

Seb sat on the bed, watching my face closely. "Well, if we're back, it will be like it was before, right?"

I twisted a piece of hair that had fallen into my face.

"Before like we've been this semester on campus, only maybe with sex, or before you left for Moo U when we were totally together?"

He didn't answer right away. "What do you want?"

I wanted him to tell me what he wanted first. But I'd been the one to cut things off last year, and I'd been the one to freak out and ghost him again here after we had sex. Yeah, he had reason to worry about what I wanted after that. I needed to push out of my crease and make my move.

"I want us to be friends." He dropped his gaze from me. "Because you're the best friend I've ever had. And I want us to have sex."

That brought his gaze back.

"Lots and lots of sex, because you're also the best I've had that way. And I want us to be exclusive, and...I want you to love me again."

That was the scary part. Seb hadn't said he loved me since he'd left Toronto.

He nodded, and I got braver about the things I wanted. He moved to lie beside me, and then his hand was in my hair, pulling me forward, and his lips were on mine. I met him kiss for kiss, tongue for tongue, and those nerves, the fears, they were gone. It was us again, and I couldn't remember what I'd been worried about.

Finally, Seb pulled back. "Yes, to all of that. And I do love you, Faith. I'm not sure I really stopped."

I ran my fingers over his face, across the thick brows over those deep-brown eyes, the cheekbones, the nose with the bump from a stick he'd taken to the face in a street hockey game, his soft lips that promised me all I'd asked for.

"I tried to stop," I admitted, not wanting to hurt him but needing to be honest. "After what I thought happened last year, I knew I had to, because I couldn't be like my mom. But there was never anyone else who could replace you."

He growled and grabbed my hand, rolling me onto my back. "I plan to make sure there never will be."

His mouth moved over my neck, using all the things he'd learned about me to make me soften, then shiver, and then move against him. His tongue circled my nipples, his hands tracing patterns on my ribs as he kept moving down, licking, biting, kissing, bringing me back to the edge.

"Seb, please," I begged.

"Say it," he growled, breath harsh.

I ran my hand over his head, brushing over his cheekbones, then his lips. "I love you."

He closed his eyes for a moment, a smile crossing his face. Then he parted my legs and kissed my thighs, moving his hands closer to my core. I focused dazed eyes to find him looking back at me, a grin on his face, and then he moved that mouth to the needy place between my legs, and I couldn't meet his gaze anymore. I couldn't do anything but squirm, try to bring him closer, and then push him away as the sensations threatened to become too much. I was gasping his name, pulling his hair, lost to everything but his mouth and the fingers that slid inside.

I was gone, again.

When I opened my eyes, Seb was still between my legs, watching me with a warm, satisfied look.

"Come up here."

He promptly crawled up my body, dropping more kisses on my sensitive skin as he did, until he was finally braced over me, face above mine. I reached for a kiss, tasting myself on him, and then, using the muscles he obviously didn't find a turnoff, I flipped him onto his back.

"My turn," I told him, my own voice growly.

I could feel his erection against my abdomen, hot and hard again, and as I slid down his body in turn, his breathing grew ragged as he figured out what I had planned.

"What are you doing, Faith?" he moaned as I grabbed his dick in a firm grasp.

"Bad things, Seb. Bad, bad things."

"Thank God." Then he stopped speaking as I took him in my mouth.

14

Sebastien

Waking up beside Faith was the best feeling ever.

I knew I had to get going soon. I had classes. She did, too. I just didn't want to break this spell. Part of me had expected her to have vanished overnight. I guess that would've been hard for her to do since we were in her room, but I was apprehensive. The sex last night had been amazing, but I still found it difficult to accept that we were good. And together. The last year had been rough.

She was wrapped tightly around her pillow, as if she had fought to keep it overnight. I had my faults, but I'd never been a cover hog, so I didn't think she was keeping it from me. Her hair was spread in blond tangles, and her face was hidden in the pillow. I thought she looked beautiful. I watched her shoulders lift and fall with her breathing, the wisps of hair moving as she exhaled. I might have been crossing the line into creeper territory here.

Her phone blared. I sat up, making myself look away.

"Seb?" Her voice was muffled with sleep, and I glanced over, willing myself to keep it together if there was any regret in her look.

"I'm here." I hoped that was what she wanted.

"I'm sleepy. Your fault."

She had her bottom lip jutting out, and I leaned over to kiss her. No regrets in those beautiful eyes. Okay, we both had morning breath, but I'd take that any day I got to wake up with Faith. My body was tired. I would pay for last night today at practice, but I didn't care. Totally worth it. Unfortunately, I couldn't brush off classes. If my GPA dropped too low, I couldn't play.

"I gotta go." I sounded reluctant. I was.

"Me, too." She looked at me, and I mentally began to calculate if I could postpone something so that I could stay here with her. How low could I let my grade point go?

She ran a finger down my nose, stopping at my lips, and I sucked it into my mouth. Sure, I could miss a couple of classes.

"So we're doing this?" she said.

I felt the grin stretching my face. No regrets, and she was still on board.

"Totally." Gripping her hand and pulling the finger out of my mouth, I reached down for another kiss. When I pulled back, she slapped a hand over her mouth.

"Don't care." I wouldn't have cared if she'd just eaten straight garlic.

She sat up, and I took a moment to enjoy the sight of a naked Faith in daylight. I hadn't had this opportunity very often previously. Before, when I'd been billeted next door to her, we'd had to find time to be together, and sex was quick and usually in the dark. This time, we'd woken up together. Slept together. I loved it, and I hoped we could do it every night. Except on weekends, when one of us would be travelling until the season ended. Shit.

"Stop staring." She bent over to grab a T-shirt and pulled it on.

I sighed. Faith's ass was a beautiful sight. But, apparently, we were getting up, so I stood up to find my own clothing. I looked over my shoulder and caught her watching *my* ass.

"Stop staring." I mock frowned at her.

"Make me."

I turned, boxers in hand, and started for her.

"No!" She raced for the bathroom and slammed the door in my face, squealing.

I promised retribution, which only made her laugh. Then I checked the time and swore, because it was late. I quickly pulled on my clothes, promised to catch up with her later, and headed back to the hockey house. I needed access to a toilet and a shower, and I needed to eat something before I had to be in class. That meant I had to rush.

Fifteen minutes later, I was back in our kitchen, assembling a smoothie with protein powder, hair wet and mind firmly back on Faith. I almost leapt when Cooper slapped my back.

"What the hell?" My heartrate was still several levels above normal.

He grinned at me. "Someone is looking very...satisfied this morning."

I felt my cheeks warm. "Uh, yeah, Faith and I are back together."

Cooper bowed with a flourish. "Then my work here is done."

"What about you? I mean, I owe you—"

He stepped back with his hands raised. "Oh no, I don't want to be paired up."

I cleared my throat. "Thanks. This... It means a lot to me." It meant everything, though I couldn't really say that. But yeah, I was in Cooper's debt, big time.

"Then you won't mind that I let Jill? Julie? Use your towel, right? She said she had to clean up."

He turned to leave while I was gaping at him.

"Have your...women use your own damn towels, Coop!"

I got only a laugh in response.

Faith

Seb was waiting when I got out of practice.

The guys were on the ice next, but I normally didn't see them.

They were in their locker room getting ready while we were on the ice. And when we were done, they headed out for their own practice. Today, Seb was standing outside our locker room waiting for me. It was sweet, and I felt a smile form on my face.

"Hey."

I got glances from some of my teammates as they headed out. I wasn't sure what they might think about this, so I started walking to the exterior doors, hoping to move Seb along. I guess if we were dating now, people were going to know. I hadn't really thought that through. I probably shouldn't worry about what my teammates thought, but even though I was getting more starts, at least as backup, I wasn't sure Coach was really on Team Devereaux. And if word got back to her...

"Shouldn't you be getting dressed to get on the ice?"

Seb shrugged. "I'll be there. Just wanted to see you first."

"Why?"

"For this." He framed my face with his hands and kissed me.

It wasn't a long, drawn-out kiss, but it packed a wallop. I heard someone whistle in the background. Seb ignored the whistle, and anyone else who might be around. He was focused on me. Only. He pulled back, and it took me a minute to remember where I was. I blinked, coming back to the here and now.

"Wanna go for pizza tonight?"

I was feeling the effects of the kiss and was still confused about how to break this news to my teammates, so I nodded and took off for class.

There was no doubt that Seb was all in. I just... I guess I hadn't thought he would be all in right away. I'd thought... I don't know what I'd thought exactly. I'd been in a cocoon of love and lust and hormones and hadn't thought about the details of what being together would be like outside my room. Part of me was on board, because this was Seb, and I loved him. I had missed him, all of him, the past year. But once I was on my own, back in the real world, there was a part of me that was still confused. There was just so much going on right now. Adjusting to college was more challenging than I'd imagined. My classes were getting better, but they weren't easy. Did I have time for dating?

When it came to hockey, I felt like I'd built some bridges, but they were temporary ones. Easily damaged. I didn't feel that confident bond with my team and coach like I had before. Maybe I was paranoid, but I felt like I was on probation. How would they react to this?

Then there was my grandmother. It was a whole lot of change, a lot of challenges, and while I was up for it—I truly was—it wasn't easy.

And now Seb.

Just one thing to focus on would've been enough, but that wasn't the play in front of me. I tried to shove all that confusion aside to get through classes, and then I came back to my room to get ready for our pizza date. But I was still on edge when Seb came to pick me up.

Penny had a smug look on her face when he showed up at our door. She'd accused me of having a glow when she saw me this morning. It hadn't been hard for her to figure out what was going on with Seb and me. I suspected we hadn't been all that quiet. I didn't know when she got back to our room, but let's just say I wasn't going to ask her what she might have heard. It didn't help that Seb blushed when Penny smirked at him. But even though she was giving me a bit of a hard time, I knew she was happy for me.

It was nice to go get pizza with Seb. This was familiar, something we'd done countless times. He slipped his hand around mine as we headed down the sidewalk, and it felt good. Right. When I was with him, those anxious thoughts went away, at least for a while. This was *Seb*. And Seb and I together were so good.

We sat at a table, and once we'd ordered, he played with my hand while we waited for the pizza. Just like he'd always done. Rubbing his fingers over mine, he traced the lines on my palm, sending tendrils of awareness through me. Every now and then, my brain would switch back to last year, and I'd tense, remembering that I hated Seb and that he was a cheater—only to remind myself that was wrong. Then I'd relax my shoulders and try to make up for the lapse by paying more attention to him. My brain was a confusing place to be right now.

We were talking hockey—how our seasons were going—when suddenly his eyes widened.

"Shit, I forgot. How's your grandma?"

I swallowed and put down my slice.

"I need to thank you. They're coming to watch me play this weekend. Mom and Gramma. That was a great idea you had. Coach is letting me start the Friday game, so Gram will get to watch me play one more time."

I had to blink my eyes. I purposely didn't say one last time, but it was still there, disguise it how I might. I didn't want to start crying. Gramma was being strong about this, so I needed to as well.

Seb reached over and squeezed my hand. "I'm glad you'll get to see her, and she'll get to watch you play."

"Me, too." My voice was rough.

"When do they arrive on campus?"

"About an hour before the game. I won't see them 'til after."

"And when are they leaving?"

"Saturday afternoon. Gramma can't stay long."

Seb's face fell. "Damn. I would've liked to see them."

It was terrible, but I felt a sense of relief. I didn't want to talk about Seb with my family.

They knew we'd been going out when he left for Burlington. And that we'd broken up. I'd told them it was because of the long-distance thing. I hadn't mentioned anything else. I hadn't wanted to talk to my mom about Seb cheating. I especially hadn't wanted to talk with my dad about it.

My dad cheated. For as long as I could remember, there'd been hushed fights, and my mom crying. I didn't understand it, not when I was young, but as I got older, my mom would tell me stuff. My dad liked to tell stories about his clients. They were all athletes, all professionals, and not all of them cheated, but he had a lot of stories about the problems he had to help them with. It seemed like a lot of the problems involved women they hooked up with. Keeping it out of the press. Paying women off. Dealing with child support when someone got pregnant. And so many of these douchebags were married. Married or seriously involved with someone, and they still messed around. Like Dad did.

So cheating was a topic we didn't talk about together. If my mom heard that Seb had cheated on me, she'd have freaked and fussed over me and blamed Dad and, yeah, it would have been a mess. One she would continue to harp on. One I wanted to avoid. But Seb didn't cheat. So how could I explain the breakup and getting back together? Would they believe it was as simple as distance no longer being a factor?

In any case, getting into anything about me dating seemed like a disaster waiting to be unleashed. My dad was big on me focusing on hockey and classes, and my mom would fuss about me getting hurt, and I just didn't need to deal with that. I wanted to focus on my grandmother.

I just made a non-committal sound and asked Seb about the team the men were playing against this weekend. If—no, *when* we'd been together for a while, I'd mention it to my family.

It was great to see Gramma.

I didn't get to see them before the game, but after, I met them in the arena lobby. I'd rushed through showering and changing. I didn't have long with them, and I didn't want to waste any time. It was a shock to see Gramma in a wheelchair. I swallowed a huge lump in my throat and hugged her carefully. She felt more fragile than when I'd left Toronto a couple of months ago.

"None of that, Faith. I don't need you to treat me like an invalid," she said, even though she was talking from her wheelchair.

"You played so well. I'm glad I got to see you. Is there some-place we can pick up some snacks? I want to talk to you, and I know you're hungry after a game."

She knew me well. And I knew where to find food. We went back to their motel room since she had to rest. I memorized every moment, every word we got to share. I stayed overnight with them and saw them off after breakfast the next day to catch their flight home. Part of me wanted to go with them. I knew I didn't have much more time with her. I wanted to treasure every minute. She said no. She wanted me to reach my dreams, and she refused to let me risk them, even for this.

I insisted I'd fly home the next weekend I wasn't playing. And I was going to spend every minute possible with her over Christmas break. That, she'd let me do. Still, I hugged her tightly before she got in the cab and fought back tears as I waved goodbye.

I wished Seb were here, just to have someone to hold me. But the men's team was out of town this weekend. They always were when we played at home. They'd head back after tonight's game. And even though I wasn't scheduled to start tonight, I was backup and needed to be ready. I went to the arena for practice and did the best I could to block my emotions as I worked out with my team.

15

Sebastien

I could tell that Faith was upset about her grandmother. She wouldn't say anything, but when I saw her on Sunday, she hugged me tightly and didn't let go for longer than normal. I was more than willing to keep her in my arms as long as she needed. I'd happily have Faith there anytime.

When she pulled herself back with a sniffle that I carefully ignored, we went for breakfast. I asked her about her game Friday night. She'd had a shutout, her second since being here. That led to talking about my games, and hockey helped us, as it had done so often. It was something we both loved.

I'd played well this weekend. Cooper and I were clicking together. Sometimes the chemistry was just there between defensive partners, and it was for us. I'd made a couple of no-look passes to him, and he'd been right where I sent the puck. I was learning how he played, where he'd be on the ice. I knew he'd move a particular way when someone was blocking him from my pass, so I could pass it to where he would be, not where he was. And it was working both ways. He knew I'd stay back, make sure our goalie had support if needed, that I'd be the first one back in our zone when play moved that way, so he was quicker to jump forward, join the forwards in the other end, which made the team a bigger threat offensively. Coach noticed.

Faith understood when I described it to her, but she wasn't a skater. She had to know how her teammates reacted so that when she blocked shots, or when there was a rush heading her way, she knew what they could do for her, and what she had to do on her own to keep the puck out of her net. But she didn't have that one-on-one chemistry with a teammate because she didn't play most of the time with one person.

The forwards could have that same kind of chemistry with their line mates as we did on defense. We had four lines of forwards, and three pairs of D-men, and others to fill in as needed. We took shifts on the ice, normally with our line mates. But goalies were on their own. They were out there with all of us. As a result, goalies were often fucking weird. Faith, not so much. I mean, I'd seen her play, and she did talk to her goalposts some-times, but she didn't have bizarre rituals in the locker room—at least, not that she'd shared. Except for her lucky hair ribbon, which she hated to be teased about.

I told her all about my assist from the last game, and her face lit up, proud of my success, just like I was proud of hers.

"You're so gonna do well in the draft if you and Cooper keep that up."

I kind of froze, because this was the first time we'd talked about the draft. At least, the first time now. We'd talked about playing professionally before the breakup. I knew it was her plan, and how much this time in college would factor in her future. She knew it was what I wanted to do, too. At least, back then. It just hadn't come up in conversation since we'd been back together.

I knew Faith assumed I was hoping to be drafted, just like everyone else here thought. Everyone but me. I was…conflicted. I'd managed to deflect everyone. Hockey players were supersti-tious in a lot of ways. Most people probably thought I didn't want to jinx anything by talking about it. Not Faith though. She knew me.

"What's wrong, Seb?"

My knee jiggled. I didn't want to risk our new relationship. On the other hand, I didn't want to deflect with Faith. I wasn't sure I could, to be honest. She saw me. She knew my family. She'd be the person most likely to understand why I was confused about this. She was maybe the only person I could share this with.

"I don't know... I don't know about being drafted."

She cocked her head and narrowed her eyes. "You have a chance, Seb. A good one. I haven't seen you play a real game in person, not this year, but I've watched some of your games online."

I wasn't looking for reassurance, but that made something warm flicker inside me. That she'd watched, and that she thought I'd played well. Because Faith was not good at empty compliments.

"I mean, if I was drafted, I don't know if I'd go."

I could see the surprise on her face. "Would it depend on what team it was?"

Not like I could pick and choose. That wasn't how it worked. I could say no to whatever team drafted me, but it meant I wouldn't play, at all.

I shook my head. The silence stretched.

"What's going on, Seb? What's changed?"

Before I'd left for Burlington for freshman year, we'd talked endlessly about playing professionally. Both of us. It was unfair, but my chances were better. I couldn't meet her gaze. I looked down at the table, putting a hand down to settle my leg.

"Unless I was drafted high, I'd probably never play. And if I did, I mean, I could be injured or something." I shrugged. "Then what?"

I shot a glance up to catch her reaction. Faith opened her mouth, shook her head, then closed her mouth again.

"What..." Then her eyes widened. "It's your fucking family, isn't it?"

I nodded. I knew Faith would get it.

"What the *fuck* have they been saying to you, Seb?"

My family wasn't horrible. They loved me, I knew, in their own way. They didn't force me to do things. They wanted good things for me. It's just that they kind of…ignored me. Most of the time.

"If I get my degree, then I can get a job and establish myself. If I go the hockey route, the odds aren't great I'll go pro, and if I do, it probably won't be for very long, so not a lot of money, and then I'd be behind everyone. And if I get a concussion or something…"

Faith had her jaw clenched tightly, and her eyes were flashing. "Come on." She grabbed her tray and headed for the exit.

I followed her. I knew she was angry, and I hoped it wasn't with me. Once we were out of the dining hall, she grabbed my hand and pulled me around a corner. On a Sunday morning, the place was deserted. She grabbed my chin and made me meet her gaze.

"Seb, your family hasn't supported you in any way except by paying places to keep you, just so they didn't have to deal with you. It was nice for them that hockey kept you out of their hair, but now they want you to give it up? No fucking way. Hockey is your dream, and you can damn well go for it."

I bit my lip, trying to work out my feelings. Faith sighed.

"Seb, you don't owe them anything. Not really. They threw money at you, sent you to hockey camps because they didn't want to deal with you. They can't start telling you what to do now. You know they're not going to change if you do what they want, right? They're not suddenly going to include you in everything, and I don't know, set aside a room for you again. This is all to make sure you take the guaranteed route so they can keep ignoring you."

I closed my eyes, hurt by the truth in her words. It wasn't that my parents were evil or hated me. But I had never really been wanted. As much as they liked their happy families, I was a reminder of the mistake they'd made. They split custody, and somehow, I never really fit in either place.

Faith was right. When I started to play hockey and was good at it, they'd been happy to send me away on school breaks to hockey camps. I'd been happy to go, because when I played well, someone was glad to have me around.

It had been nice to be wanted, at least by a team. I knew Faith was right, but it was hard. I'd tried all my life to make them want me around. I'd been well-behaved, helped out, was never difficult. I'd never gotten into any trouble, but somehow, I was still too much for them.

We, my mom and dad and I, discussed things like where I was supposed to be and when. How school was. How my hockey team did—they never looked it up themselves. General how-are-things-going conversation. Most of the time, they didn't ask what I wanted or what my dreams were.

They'd been happy I'd gotten a scholarship to college to play hockey. I mean, I knew they'd have helped with tuition at least. They always did what they were supposed to and split the costs right down the middle. But as they said, they had other kids that would need that money later. The money that they didn't have to pay for my college tuition.

They liked the idea of me with a regular career. One that would leave me self-sufficient. Not a burden. And the kid inside me, the one who'd always wanted them to want me, wanted to do what they asked. To try to fucking please them.

Faith was right. That was never going to happen. I hadn't wanted to face it.

I pulled Faith into a tight embrace. Really tight. With other girls I'd dated, I might have needed to hold back, but Faith wasn't tiny and fragile. She was strong and loyal and here. And I loved her. I'd never stopped, and I'd do anything to make sure we survived together this time.

Anything.

Faith

I had a boyfriend again. Seb. Again.

I'd had my doubts. Partly because I was rewiring my brain now that I knew he hadn't cheated. And partly because I'd planned to *not* be involved with anyone. I knew I needed to focus on my game and my classes. I'd been afraid getting involved with someone would mean I wouldn't keep up with the other stuff.

Seb was helping me with my classes. Not that he was a genius or straight A student, but he had a year of experience, and he knew me. He could say something, and it would open a door in my brain and things would make more sense. And being involved with someone in hockey helped in a way I hadn't considered. Most of the time, goalies were the oddballs of the team. We tended to be a little more superstitious, and we were in the minority. Our training was a little different. And while I was working hard on bonding with the team, I was having more problems with the other two goalies.

I wanted to replace Anderson, and everyone knew that. That was the normal dynamic. On my last team, I'd been the starter, and my backup had wanted my spot. But we'd gotten along well, because, without bragging, I was a lot better than she was. I'd wanted to help her so the team would be in good shape when I left.

Anders wasn't better than me. Not really. I understood this was her last year, and maybe her last time to be a hockey player, but I also wanted to play, and I really wanted to win. Unlike me and my backup last year, she didn't reach out to me. I didn't know her reasons, but I suspected she was afraid I might push her into being the backup.

Our other freshman goalie, Vash, was even worse. She'd hoped to be the next starter, and I was way better than she was. I'd offered to work with her, but she'd started refusing. She and Anders had formed a partnership. They worked together, and I was left out. It wasn't a happy situation, at least not for me.

Having Seb to talk hockey with, even while he couldn't talk

goalie things with me, helped. Proving what a great guy he was, Seb invited their freshman goalie to eat with us a few times, so I had someone to get into goalie details with. Talking to Briggs about what the men's team was doing with him was awesome, and I added some things to my own workouts as a result. That was all good.

The sex was awesome. I think I'd blanked that part of our relationship out because it hurt too much to remember. Or maybe we'd both gotten better at it. I didn't dwell on what might have happened this last year to make it feel that way. One of us was always out of town on the weekends, but we got together Sundays, and we spent most of our weeknights together. And it was great.

Word got out about us being together, obviously. I was worried about what Coach would think. We were getting along better, but I still felt like she was waiting for me to prove myself. Not on the ice, because when I got to play, I played really well. I based that on my save percentage, my GAA, my wins, and by the way my teammates played when I was in net. Our defense played more loosely, not worrying that I couldn't cover things behind them. They could jump in on rushes, and it helped the whole team.

Coach didn't appear to place much stock in that.

I was also doing everything I needed to in practice. I was mostly shut out by the other two goalies, but for weight training, cardio, and on-ice drills, I did everything I was asked. I was one of the first to arrive, and one of the last to leave. Every single practice. But I wasn't getting a lot of starts. I was mostly sitting there as backup, and I still felt like Coach was waiting for me to do something to show I wasn't a part of the team.

Then at the beginning of December, on a Saturday away game, that message was hammered home. We'd played well and won on Friday night, but nothing was working Saturday. Everyone seemed a little on edge. Everything was just a little off, from our morning skate to our pre-game warmup. Then the game started, and everything went to hell. Our forwards couldn't make a pass to save themselves. The defense was out of position, Anders was left high and dry, and she was as off as everyone else. Part way through the third, when the score was six zero against us, Coach finally put me in.

I'd been off today as well, and sitting on the bench after we went down three zero in the first, I'd moved from frustrated to irritated to angry to furious. I didn't blame the score on our goalie. This was a team game—we won or lost as a team. But sometimes, when everything is going wrong, the coach needs to shake things up to get the team working right again. In the pros, a fight can do that. We couldn't fight in our games. A goal can also change how a team plays, but we weren't getting those. Another thing the coach can do is put in the backup goalie.

I mean, if I were in net and got four scored on me before the game was half over, I'd want out. I'd want to do something. It seemed that when Coach was so desperate that she had no other option, she put me in, too late to make a difference. All the waiting and getting angry had fixed whatever was wrong with me, because when I got out there, things were right again. At least for me. It did help the team. I shut the door on any more goals against us, and we somehow managed to get a couple scored. But it was past the point where we could save the game.

Afterwards, my teammates were great. We all told Anders it wasn't her fault, but I got some taps, letting me know they knew I'd done well. I rushed through my shower and got out of there as soon as I could. I found a seat at the back of the bus and put on headphones, not wanting to talk, not wanting to make eye contact. I was pissed. And frustrated. I wasn't sure what else I could do for Coach.

I texted Seb. I needed to vent to someone, and the men's game had ended already. They'd won, so Seb should be in a good mood. The rest of the team loaded up on the bus, and fortunately, no one sat with me. I turned my music up loud and waited for Seb to answer.

And waited.

And waited.

My foot was jiggling, my fists were clenched, and no dots showed up on the phone. Seb wasn't a guy who played games, timing how quickly he responded to a text as a power play. I'd gotten a good-luck text from him before the game, even though I hadn't been scheduled to start. He'd know by now that we'd lost. He'd know why I was reaching out. But he didn't answer.

My foot was jiggling faster, but I was a rational person, and I knew there could be a reason why he couldn't respond. After half an hour, though, the reasons were starting to look bad. I double-checked the results from the men's game. No injuries, Seb had played almost until the last shift. No notices that he'd fallen in the shower and hit his head.

Still, I was getting worried. My thumbs flew over the keyboard as I did whatever research I could online to find out what was happening. I finally found a picture. Of Seb. After the game. At a party at the hockey house.

I could live with him going to parties without me. It wasn't like he could skip one at the hockey house since it was his home. And since we were never together on weekends, I wouldn't expect him to stay in his room alone. His team had won an important game. Of course they'd celebrate.

He could have turned off his notifications, or he might not have heard or noticed his phone with a noisy group at the house.

I mean, I could make that narrative work. If I tried. But he was with a girl in the photo. A tiny, pretty brunette, and his head was down while hers was tilted up. From that angle, you couldn't see exactly what was happening, but it was easy to imagine possibilities.

Like he was kissing her.

16

Faith

I closed my eyes and counted to fifty. Then I made myself stop that self-destructive loop that immediately started saying he was cheating. Again. I reminded myself he hadn't cheated the last time, and if I'd given him a chance to explain, we'd both have avoided a lot of heartache. I didn't know everything that was going on. He would have an explanation.

I refused to let myself look for more pictures. I wasn't going to be suspicious and crazy. I wasn't going to be like my mother when she was sure my dad was cheating.

No, I was going to be a grown-up. An adult.

We were due to get in late tonight, so Seb and I had arranged to meet in the morning. I would do that. I would let him explain why he hadn't responded to me, and what happened in that picture. Assuming he didn't reach out before then, which he totally would, because this was Seb. He wasn't like my dad.

We got back to campus late, slowed by bad driving conditions. We unloaded our stuff, and my phone didn't buzz. I made it to my room, keeping quiet so that Penny didn't wake up. No message yet.

I didn't fall asleep for a long time, and my phone was quiet all night.

———————

Sebastien

The team were all a little goofy since we'd won a hard game against our most difficult opponent on home ice. It was a squeaker, too. The score didn't show that, since we scored two goals in the last five minutes, but the adrenaline was buzzing. I saw that Faith's game was not going well, so thought I'd wait until it was done before I sent her a message about how well our game had gone. We all had to shake off those bad games, and everyone deserved a bit of time to dwell and feel bad.

Normally, we hit up Biscuit in the Basket after a game. We younger guys couldn't get any alcohol at the bar unless someone charmed the wait staff, but it was a tradition. It was probably good that we didn't drink after every game anyway. Tonight though, my roommates thought we should have a party at the hockey house because it was Marcher's birthday, and his best friend and his sister, who were dating, had come up for the game. So yeah, we had to have a party.

When I'd insisted I needed to go up to my room and talk to Faith for a bit, Cooper had picked me up, thrown me over his shoulder to carry me back, and since he wasn't much taller or heavier than me, he'd managed to knock my phone out of my pocket and into someone's abandoned cup of beer just before he dropped me.

It took five minutes before he believed I had to go back and rescue it, and by then, it wasn't responding. I cleaned it with fresh water best I could and dropped it in a bag of rice. While I was doing that, Marcher introduced me to his sister, Raylene. She was going to school in Toronto, and Marcher had told her that I had lived there and might be able to direct her to the best places to go to eat and meet people. I tried, but the place was loud, and she talked so quietly I almost had to bend over to hear what she was saying. We finally went out on the porch to hear ourselves talk.

I asked if I could use her phone to text Faith, but she had some weird plan that wouldn't let her text in the US. Cell phone packages were a lot more expensive up in Canada, I remembered, so I couldn't blame her. We went back in, and I checked my phone again. Nothing. I needed to borrow another phone, but Cooper had started some stupid games, and by the time I could break away, it was too late to reach out to Faith. I felt badly that I hadn't got a hold of her, but we were meeting for breakfast, and I'd explain then. Still, it would be good to leave her a message to see when she woke up.

As we were finally cleaning up, I insisted that Cooper let me use his phone. But he'd been taking pictures and videos all night, and it was out of battery. He was drunk, had no idea where his charger was, and passed out on his bed before he found it.

Shit. Her team had a bad game, and I should have done more to reach out to her. So what if the guys would've given me grief for needing to speak to her? I hadn't wanted to use their phones because I didn't want them to have her number. Not that I thought they'd have tried anything with her, but because who the hell knew what stupid stuff they'd send her. Now I thought I should have risked it.

I'd apologize as soon as I saw her.

Cellphones are important for more than music and messaging and looking up stupid shit online. Mine was my alarm, and unsurprisingly, it didn't reach out from the bag of rice and wake me up. We'd gone to bed late because of the party, and it was Sunday, our day off, so without any annoying noise, I slept in.

I couldn't even call Faith to tell her I was running late, so I had to do some quick calculations. I sniffed my pits and decided I could skip a shower. I pulled on some clothes, not paying a lot of attention to what I was wearing, anxious to see Faith. I grabbed the baggie full of rice and phone and ran, literally, to find her in the campus dining room we'd planned to eat in. I hoped she didn't think I'd stood her up.

We were back together, but it was still kind of new. I didn't want to mess things up, not again, and this whole fuck up since the game last night wasn't good. Faith was just leaving the dining room when I ran up, and I knew I was in trouble. I pulled out the rice bag with my phone, wanting to present my excuse before she could get any more upset.

"Sorry, sorry, sorry, Faith! I'm so sorry! My phone got soaked in beer, so I couldn't call you, and that meant I didn't have an alarm, so I slept in." I was panting so hard I wasn't sure she'd understood me. Her expression was closed, her arms crossed.

Damn it, I should have sent a text without waiting for her game to be over. Texting her when she was upset about a bad game would have been so much better than this extended silence. I knew it was too easy for her to take something like this the wrong way because of how screwed up her parents were. I should have borrowed anyone's phone.

She stared at me for too long. *Shit.* But sometimes things happened. She had to give me a chance. She had to. After last time, she'd let me explain, right?

"I swear, Faith, I've been trying to get this thing working since right after I got home last night. It's not my fault. I totally meant to call you." I waited, trying to read her expression, but she wasn't showing much.

Finally, she shrugged. "Okay, let's eat."

I felt the air rush out of my lungs. I was so relieved she wasn't going to cut me off without a chance to explain like last year. I could tell I wasn't totally out of the woods, so I refrained from kissing her. For now.

She must have eaten already, because she grabbed a table while I got some food. Well, a lot of food, because hockey took up a lot of energy. I shot glances her way, but she just stared at the table, face closed off.

I was sweaty from running over, and I'd dressed in such a hurry that my T-shirt was on backwards and the tag was irritating my throat. I couldn't very well strip off my clothes to fix it, so it just made me irritable. It was a shitty start to the day, but I could turn it around. I just had to explain to Faith, then we could go back to the hockey house, and I could shower and put my clothes on right and things would be good. We could hang out today like we'd planned to do.

I shot another glance at Faith and told myself to be patient. This was the first problem that had come up since we'd gotten back together. I should be relieved that she hadn't totally freaked and was giving me a chance. But part of me was annoyed. I'd done nothing wrong. In fact, Cooper had only started horsing around, causing me to lose my phone, because I'd been trying to get a hold of her. I could already tell these next few days until I got this one replaced were going to be a pain. I didn't have a lot of confidence in the powers of rice to fix it after it had spent five minutes in cheap beer. It had been about twelve hours since I'd rescued it, and the stupid thing was still dead.

As I returned to the table, I forced myself to calm down, slow my breathing, and figure out what I was going to say. Faith might be mad I hadn't messaged her, and I understood why she was a little touchy about it, but we had to be able to get through things like this. Maybe this would help her trust me going forward.

I set my tray on the table across from her and then pulled out the rice baggie again. After I sat down, I opened the bag so I could access the phone and try to turn it on. Nothing happened. Great. Fucking great. I swallowed a gulp of coffee, irritated that Faith hadn't said anything yet.

I nudged the phone. "This fell in a cup of beer."

I took a mouthful of eggs, because I was definitely hungry. Hungry was better than irritated.

Faith picked it up, examined it, and tried to turn it on as well.

I swallowed. "You'll be shocked to hear that it was Cooper's fault."

Her mouth turned up just a bit. Okay, we'd get through this.

"I'm sorry, Faith. I was actually going upstairs to call you when Cooper decided I couldn't leave the party, and that stupidity resulted in my phone dropping in a cup of beer. I know your game was a bust. How's the team doing? How are you?"

I could be a good boyfriend. I liked being in a relationship, and I was willing to do the work.

She shrugged. "Coach put me in during the third. We were down six zero. It was too late."

I understood. I'd been able to catch the score and knew Faith had shut the door, and the team had scored a couple of goals. If she'd been put in earlier, it might have changed things.

"I'm sorry." Sorry that her coach still didn't trust her, not completely. I wasn't going to mention our game. No one needed someone else's success rubbed in, and it seemed like Faith had not gotten over the team's loss yet. She was taking it hard, still quiet and frowning.

She nudged my phone again. I ate some more, since I was hungry, and I thought it was up to her now. I'd apologized for not reaching out. I'd asked about her game. I didn't know what else I was supposed to do.

"You okay?" Something was obviously wrong. Was it the game and her coach? How upset was she that I hadn't called? I was trying to be understanding, but this was a little much. Maybe I needed to be more patient.

She glanced up at me, her expression not a happy one. She looked…pissed. But I had no idea why.

"Do you have anything else to say?"

I had my fork halfway to my mouth, but I froze. "Faith, I

meant to call you. I tried to get out of the noise and ended up with my phone in a cup of beer, and now I'm without a phone, and I can already tell this is going to be a problem. I don't have an alarm, which is why I was late to breakfast. I'm sorry for all that, but I did try. I even asked to borrow someone else's phone, but she couldn't do texts in the US. And then it was late, and I didn't want to disturb you. What else do you want?"

Faith's mouth clamped shut. She pulled out her own phone, swiped a few times, and then she set it on the table and shoved it over to me. There was a photo on the screen, one someone had posted on Insta from the party last night. It was me and Raylene, and I could see how it could look suspicious.

I mean, if someone leaning over to possibly kiss someone on their cheek got you riled up. I had been trying to talk into her ear, I wasn't near her mouth. I sat up, ready to explain to Faith that Raylene was Marcher's sister and had been there for his birthday, and that she was dating the guy standing on the other side of her. I was pretty sure if you looked through Raylene's account, you'd find a shit ton of pictures of the two of them together, because that's how girls liked to do Insta—at least, my exes had.

Faith had her arms crossed, and she didn't look at me. She had already decided I'd cheated. Or almost cheated. Or wanted to. I could prove I hadn't...this time. This time, the girl happened to have her boyfriend right beside her, and if I needed, I could get everyone from the party to back up my story. From the way Faith was looking, I might have to. It would be embarrassing, but I could definitely make them do it. This time, I could. But what about the next time?

The truth was, I was a hockey player. And people liked to take pictures with hockey players. Sometimes, they liked to pretend it was more than just a shot with a fan. They wanted a picture that looked like they'd been close to a hockey player. The way things were here at Moo U, there were going to be a lot of those occasions where Faith wouldn't be around. I couldn't always show that a girl in a photo had a boyfriend. There might not be people around who could vouch for me and give me an alibi. And what if I did go pro, like she'd encouraged me? It would only get worse. More women, more photos, more stories.

I imagined a series of confrontations like this in the future. Faith with a picture or story, asking me to prove I hadn't cheated. A lifetime of being like her parents. Except I hadn't done anything wrong, and I was still in trouble. Was this how it had started with her parents? Would we always have a relationship disrupted by accusations and defenses? It would look just like her home life. A chill slid under the sweat I'd worked up while running over here to placate Faith.

I couldn't do it. I wouldn't always be able to provide proof. *This* had been pretty innocuous, and it wouldn't take much work to discover the truth. And yet *this* was a problem. It wasn't going to work.

We weren't going to work.

I hadn't understood before just how deeply her parents had affected her. She was always going to need proof. And what about the time I didn't have it? I knew what would happen. Exactly what had happened last year. She'd be gone.

I couldn't eat another bite. Last year had been brutal. Going through it over and over again? Eventually, Faith would be gone permanently.

I set down my fork, reached for my phone, and carefully sealed it back up in the baggie. It was probably as lost a cause as we were, but leaving it on the table was pointless. I put it in my jacket pocket.

I stood up. "I didn't do anything wrong, Faith. I wouldn't."

She blinked her eyes, fast, and I knew there were tears. "Then tell me. Prove it."

"I could do that this time. But I shouldn't have to. And what about the next time? What about when I can't?"

She wouldn't look at me. I could feel the pain spreading out from the middle of my chest, making my hands and knees shake.

"Goodbye, Faith."

It wasn't just goodbye for now, I knew that. I blinked back my own tears and tried to swallow over a lump the size of a puck in my throat. I walked out, away from the girl I loved. But better now than after we ruined that love. My head knew that.

My heart didn't.

17

Faith

I read something once about a woman who was stabbed but didn't feel it. She walked down the dock and onto a boat or something and fell down dead later. This was kind of like that. Seb walked away, I put the tray and dishes in their proper places and went back to my room. No, I wasn't dead, but I was definitely wounded. There was pain coming.

How the hell had I let this happen to me again? How stupid was I?

Penny knocked on my door. I ignored her. If I kept my mind blank, I could stay numb for a while yet.

"Faith! Faith?" Penny was standing in front of me. I blinked at her. I had no idea what time it was.

"Are you okay?"

I shook my head, because I wasn't. There were probably some good reasons I shouldn't admit that, but if I was going to stay numb, I couldn't look for them.

Penny sat beside me and wrapped an arm around me. "I'm worried about you. You've been in here, so quiet... Your phone's been ringing, and you didn't answer it."

I grabbed for my phone. Maybe Seb had gone to get proof.

Maybe that goodbye hadn't meant... But it wasn't Seb who'd called. And pain sliced through the numbness I'd been embracing. I curled over with my hands wrapped around my waist. Penny kept her arm around me and offered Kleenex. That's when I knew I was crying. For me, for Seb, for my Gramma... They were knots of pain I did my best to cry out. I finally ran out of tears.

Penny was rubbing my back. "What happened, Faith? Should I call someone?"

I shook my head. And snuffled. "Seb cheated again."

She gasped. "Oh, I'm so sorry, sweetie. Wait, I thought he didn't cheat before. I'm confused."

I blew my nose and sat up. "Yeah. I forgot. It doesn't matter anyway, because this time..."

Penny had a frown creasing her forehead. "Wow. I thought he was crazy about you."

So did I. I picked up my phone again and showed her the picture. She took it, tapped on it, and used her fingers to make it bigger. I didn't watch. I'd start crying again, and I'd finally got through enough of the hurt to be angry. I needed angry if I was going to get through this.

"Faith, are you sure about this?" Her voice was cautious.

I blinked burning eyes at Penny. "What do you mean?"

She was staring at the phone, looking at a different picture now.

"Well, this is the girl in the picture you showed me." She looked up at me. "It looks like he's bending down to do something, but I don't think he was kissing her."

"Maybe not in that photo."

"That's what I mean. Unless... Is he into kinky stuff? Threesomes?"

It took me a minute to catch up with her, because my mind was somewhere else. "What?"

"This picture, the one I'm looking at now, is the same girl with this guy, and he's tagged as her boyfriend. And he's in that picture with Seb as well, right beside her. So either he was trying to kiss her with her boyfriend right there, or they're doing something else together. Is this the cheating you were talking about?"

I shook my head and grabbed the phone again. I switched between the two pictures, hands shaking. When I looked at the picture with Seb and the girl again, I could see he wasn't kissing her, not unless he was kissing her ear or something. I hadn't looked close enough the first time, and I hadn't wanted to torture myself with it after that.

Seb had been snapped leaning down by her face. It probably wasn't anything, just a strange angle. The guy beside the girl was big and built and good-looking, and he was her boyfriend.

So...I'd leapt to the wrong conclusion. I closed my eyes. *What had I done?*

Penny smiled at me. "So maybe you're wrong. I mean, unless he's into that kind of thing, and you have rules or something that he broke. I don't know anything about that, but I'd love to hear about it, if you don't mind—"

I held out a hand to cut her off. "No kink. No threesomes."

Her face fell, and I wondered if there was more to Penny than I'd realized.

"And I did talk to Seb."

Her brow creased. "So he did kiss her?"

I stared at the wall. I tried to remember what he'd actually said. I was able to hear the words now, not interpret everything through my hurt.

"He said he didn't do anything wrong. And that he shouldn't have to prove it."

Penny's mouth twisted. "He has a point. I mean, I'm on your side, obviously. But that doesn't mean you don't do stupid things."

Wasn't that the truth.

"I get it. For a year, you thought that he'd cheated. But he didn't, right?"

I nodded slowly. Obviously, I didn't have film of his whole evening, and he could have done anything, but the thing that had tripped me up was the picture, and it was turning into a big nothing.

"He has a point. You probably shouldn't accuse him of cheating just because of a picture like that, not unless there's more. He's a hockey player. Girls are always going to be trying to score with him. And they'll try to take pictures with him, and some will try to make it look like something has happened so they can tell their friends it did. Even if it didn't."

Yes. That was the reason for not dating an athlete.

"He didn't text me." My voice was small. If that silence hadn't made me suspicious and sent me looking through social media to find out what was going on, would it have made a difference?

"Was he supposed to?"

"He always answers. And this time, he didn't."

Her face was pinched up in Yoda mode. "Okay, I get it. Did he say why?"

I nodded. "His phone fell in a cup of beer at the party last night."

Penny huffed a breath. "Was that the truth?"

I flashed back to the phone in the bag of rice. The phone had smelt like beer and was very, very dead.

I nodded. "He brought the phone with him and showed me."

"Ah, sweetie. Just too much all at once, huh? Well, maybe you both just need some space, and then you can talk it through."

She was right. I needed to do some thinking, but on my own. I was shaken, first by thinking Seb had really cheated, since he wouldn't defend himself, then by realizing that I'd been very stupid, and that would take some work to understand.

My mother called again, so I pretended to agree with Penny. I said I had a paper due, thanked her for the talk, and said I needed to speak to my mom and then get to it. I could see the relief on her face. She hadn't signed up for a counselling session. She left the room, closing the door behind her so I could talk.

I managed to swipe to answer just before it went to voicemail again. "Sorry, Mom, things were—"

They were some things I really didn't want to share with her. But she didn't wait for me to finish.

"Faith, your grandmother passed away this morning."

Penny got back into helper mode, and we made all the arrangements I needed. My parents had booked a plane ticket for me. I got hold of Coach, and I wished she was more disappointed that I had to leave. Absence was arranged for my classes, and Penny found a friend of a friend who had a car and got me to the airport.

I didn't tell Seb.

I blocked out the sadness I felt about my grandmother by thinking about Seb. I'd been wrong. He hadn't cheated, hadn't done anything but lose his damn phone in some beer and not find another way to message me. Was I that needy that a guy couldn't enjoy a party with his team after a victory without me immediately thinking the worst?

Apparently.

He had a point. He wouldn't be able to prove himself innocent every time. Unless I put a tracker on him, or hired a PI or something, I was going to have to trust that he wasn't going to be tempted by the bodies that would be available to him.

Right now, we were only apart for a night or two a week. If he was drafted and started to play professionally, we'd be apart a lot more than that. I pretty much had to stay here in Burlington and finish my four years if I wanted to get on a good team.

Even professional women hockey players needed a job to be able to support playing on a team. We didn't get paid the big money like the men did. I needed my degree. He didn't. If he was drafted, he could be called up anytime. Which meant long-distance again, and he'd be an even more desirable target. I didn't like it, and my dad's voice filled my head. He'd played. He represented players. He knew what it was like. These guys were offered money, sex, fame—it was part of what they'd worked for.

Over the years, my dad had shared details about his work, and so often those details were about guys getting in trouble. And so often it was because of sex.

But Seb could be different, couldn't he?

There were some guys on his team who had girlfriends long term, and they were good. Adler was with Maggie, and JD was with Ryann. I'd met them briefly, but I didn't know them well enough to ask personal information, like did the guys ever mess around, and were they okay with that? They probably were fine, just nice, normal couples where one of them was a hockey player.

Maybe if I gave it a chance. Didn't look at pictures, didn't count the time between my texts and his, didn't listen to the rumors and the talk... I could just shut out everything. Keep myself in a bubble. But that would be stupid. Even if it were possible, I wouldn't want to be kept in the dark. I loved my mom, but I'd never be like her, so dependent on my dad that she'd accept that disrespect. I wasn't going to do that.

I'd been right all along. Dating was a distraction. I couldn't be worrying about what Seb was doing all the time. I needed to focus on hockey and school. And someday, if I wanted to risk a relationship, it would be with a guy who came home every day. Someone who didn't have women throwing themselves at him. Someone it wouldn't be a risk to trust.

Sebastien

I loved being part of my team. I was tighter with this group of guys than I was with my family. Having bonds like that was great. Until it wasn't.

After leaving Faith, I went for a run. I pushed myself, music loud in my headphones, and got back to the hockey house sweating, lungs heaving, and legs shaking. I came out of the shower to find Cooper sitting at my desk, looking through my homework assignment.

"What the fuck, man?"

He didn't look embarrassed, the way he should. He shook his head, like he was my professor. "Your handwriting is shitty."

I stalked over and slammed my notepad closed. "Thanks for sharing that totally unwanted opinion. Now get the fuck out."

Instead, he leaned back and crossed his arms behind his head. "What's wrong?"

I was not interested in talking. "Go away."

"Not 'til you tell me what's wrong."

"Who says anything is wrong?"

"You and I got more ice time last night than we've had all year. We won against a team who's ahead of us in the standings. You went to be with your girlfriend, and I didn't expect to see you again until tonight. Instead, you come back here without your girl and go for a run. A run you didn't need. I've spent enough time with you that I know how you work, Hunter. What's wrong?"

I flopped down on the bed. Might as well tell him. It wasn't going to be a secret. "Faith and I broke up."

Cooper dropped his casual pose and sat upright. "What the fuck is it with you two? What happened? Was it the phone thing? Honestly, it's like you want to end up dead in a tomb."

"The phone problem didn't help. But it was mostly a picture of me with Raylene."

Cooper stood up. "I should get extra credit for this. I'll talk to her. You didn't do anything."

I held up a hand. "Actually, I did."

Cooper's eyes widened.

"No, not that, shithead. But I'm the one who broke up with Faith." That was what happened, right? I'd been upset, and I didn't remember everything I said.

Cooper looked pissed, but he wasn't the one with his heart broken. "After all the work I did to get you two together? You just tossed it?"

I nodded.

He almost said something flippant, I could see it. Instead, he stayed quiet, watching me. "Why?" This time, his voice was low and searching. This time, he was really asking.

I stared up at the ceiling. "Her dad cheats. And he's a sports agent, and he travels, and he tells stories about all his clients and how they cheat. That's what Faith grew up with. She's suspicious. She's always going to suspect the worst."

Cooper sat back down. "Okay, her dad's a shit. But last night, I screwed up your phone, and you didn't cheat. I can probably get everyone at the party to back that up."

I appreciated it. "I know. I thought about it. But what about next time?"

"Is there going to be a next time?" He sounded shocked, which was totally stupid, because he knew better than anyone what it was like to be a successful hockey player on this campus.

"There won't be a time while we're playing hockey that we don't travel? That bodies aren't offered, and people don't take pictures and come on to us? There won't be one time where there's no way to prove that I didn't say yes to an offer?"

I could see it sinking in. He shook his head slowly.

"One of these days, Faith is going to find something or hear something. And she's going to suspect the worst, and I won't be able to prove my innocence. I see that coming. I don't know when, but it's coming. It's like playing Russian roulette. I can't always beat the odds.

"How many times am I going to have to prove that I'm not a fucking scumbag? How's that going to work?" Faith asking if I'd cheated with that expression in her eyes like she really thought I was that kind of douchebag hurt. A lot.

"Fuck." Cooper was finally catching up.

"Fuck is right. Eventually, it's going to make whatever we have ugly. I'd rather just cut the cord now." I wished my voice hadn't broken when I said that.

Cooper stood up. "Get dressed. You've run yourself into the ground, now it's time to drink yourself into oblivion. Unless…"

He had a thoughtful look, and for a minute, I thought he might have a solution. "What if she got you a cock cage?"

I gaped at him.

"It's a chastity device." He said it like he thought the issue was that I didn't know what the fucking thing was.

"I'm not— We're not—" My cheeks were as hot as I could remember them.

He laughed. "If you could see your face!"

I swore at him. He left, promising to be back in five. I knew he was just trying to add some humor and distract me. But while it had certainly shocked me, it hadn't solved the basic problem. The problem wasn't whether my dick ever went into someone's hand or mouth or pussy. I could promise not to do that and keep my promise. The problem was that Faith didn't trust me. And that was as much a mental problem as a physical one.

18

Faith

Funerals suck, but at least they keep you busy so you don't sit and cry for days.

Gramma had started to prepare for her passing, but she didn't have a lot of strength left. Since her stroke, she'd spent all her time fighting to regain her normal, but her normal had been gone. And now so was she.

The whole process made me want to just tick a box for cremation and have the fussing done with, but the planning kept Mom sane. Picking out clothes, selecting Bible verses and music, going through photos and getting some printed for the wake. Taking calls, accepting casseroles and desserts. There was a lot to keep my hands busy. I just wished it kept my brain busy, too.

I cried for Gramma and for the time I'd never get to spend with her. Sometimes the crying was for me and the stuff with Seb, but no one knew, and no one judged me, except for me.

I guess it was a nice service. I don't know what the standards are for funerals. No disasters and some tears? I was up front and didn't notice who was there and what went on for the most part. It didn't seem real. Then we stood, the interminable ritual almost over, and turned to follow the casket out. At least we didn't have to go to the graveyard. We were having an unusually cold December, and the ground was frozen. I was trying to calculate how many more minutes before this would all be over when I saw him.

Seb.

He was sitting in the back pew dressed in a dark suit. I blinked, sure I was making this up, but he was still there. That was definitely unreal. I had to pinch myself to be sure I was awake.

I had no idea how he knew about Gramma dying, since I didn't tell him. I didn't understand why he'd come all this way. My mom nudged me to keep going, since I'd stopped in my tracks. I moved my gaze away and tried to cool my face as I followed my dad out of the church.

I know we said something to Seb when he came up and offered his condolences. I was a robot at that point and had no idea what the words were. I'd never told my family we'd started dating again, and I would definitely never talk to them about anyone I was involved with when it would bring up the issue of cheating. My parents had already had a fight since I'd been home. My mom had accused my dad of not responding to her calls quickly enough this week. He'd said his phone was out of battery, and she'd accused him of being distracted by someone else.

They always did this, but this week? When Gramma had just died and was being buried? Tacky didn't begin to cover it. I hated when they did this. I wished my mom would leave him.

Back when I'd started high school and figured out what was going on, I'd asked her why she stayed. She'd said it was worth it for the family. My hockey was expensive, and she hadn't worked since they'd gotten married. What she'd said, without spelling it out for me, was that part of why she stayed was so that my life would be easier. I'd told her I'd be fine, but she'd waved me off. I'd finally had to accept it was her decision, but, wow, our family was fucked up. It was something Seb and I had in common.

I had to stop thinking things like that.

It seemed to take forever, but we could finally stop making

polite small talk with people we didn't know, Gramma's friends and my father's business associates. People had told us story after story about how wonderful Gramma was. I couldn't see Seb and wasn't sure when he'd left, but now it was just us and the funeral home people.

I was exhausted. Physically, which surprised me because I was an athlete. Mentally and emotionally, sure. That made sense. But my whole body felt at its limit. When we got back home, I pleaded fatigue and went to my room. I heard my mom ask my dad why somebody was at the service, and I could sense the fight coming on. I shut my bedroom door, chucked off the black dress and heels I'd been confined in all day, and pulled on my baggiest, softest pajamas. I put on my headphones and fell asleep to the sound of music, rather than my parents' cutting words.

I only had a week back at Moo U before the holiday break. I probably could have just stayed in Toronto, but I needed to get away. My parents weren't speaking, and our house was not a nice place to be, so I insisted on returning to school. I went nowhere but the arena and my classes. I was still coming to terms with Gramma's death, and my professors and the team sympathized and all did their best to make things go smoothly for me. Mostly though, I wanted to avoid Seb.

Seb, who'd somehow come all the way to Canada for the funeral. That confused me so much, because he'd been the one to say goodbye. He could have reassured me, proven that he hadn't cheated, but he'd chosen not to do so. Maybe it was a test I'd failed. I didn't really want to know.

I just wanted to get through finals and pour out everything I could on the rink. Maybe when I went back home, I'd finally have enough time and mental bandwidth to figure out what the fuck was going on and what I was doing. Hopefully, my parents wouldn't create a war zone for the holidays.

I had two weeks off for Christmas break, so the odds were not in my favor.

Sebastien

I wasn't looking forward to the Christmas break, but it was also a relief. Avoiding someone was tiring, and I was stressed enough making sure not to be where Faith was that Cooper noticed. And being Cooper, he gave me a hard time about it.

"You said you were done with her."

"I know."

"So why the fuck did you go to Canada for her grandmother's funeral?"

There was a difference between saying you're done with someone and actually being over them. Not that Cooper would know. It had been dumb to go, undoubtedly, but I'd run across Faith's roommate Penny a couple of days after our...breakup? That didn't seem like the right word. There'd been no fireworks, no big fight...just a fizzling out. Neither of us had fought.

It was depressing. Maybe I was wrong. Maybe I should have...

I just didn't know.

I couldn't just fall out of love with Faith. She'd become part of me years ago. She was the first person I'd opened up to. And when we'd gotten back together, it had been like a missing piece of me was back in place. Getting over her was going to take a long time.

When I'd run into Penny just after that last talk with Faith, I'd asked her how Faith was doing. There would always be a connection between Faith and me, a lot of emotion, and it had to mess with her like it did me. I hadn't been sure what I would do with any answer Penny gave me. If Faith was upset, was it supposed to make me feel better that it hurt her as well, or worse, because her hurting hurt me? If she was doing okay, that wasn't going to help me. No one wanted to feel replaceable. Though at least I had some experience with that.

But Penny had told me Faith's grandmother had died, and she'd gone back for the funeral, and that had gutted me. She was hurting, and the people who cared about her should gather around to help and support her. I hadn't known it, but I'd left her when she needed someone most.

I'd had my phone out, ready to call her, when reality had slapped me upside the head. I couldn't undo what I'd said and done, and neither could she. Instead of calling her, I'd opened a browser and looked for information on her grandmother's funeral.

Cooper thought I was an idiot, and maybe he was right, but I'd asked Coach for some compassionate leave, spoken to my profs, borrowed a car and taken a couple of days off to drive up to Canada and be there at the funeral. It had ended up a bust. I didn't even touch Faith, hardly spoke to her. But I'd tried.

Her grandmother had been a really nice woman, and being there for Faith had felt right. If Faith had given a sign, anything, I'd have done whatever she needed. Given hugs, been a shoulder to cry on, brought ice cream—I didn't know what the right thing was when someone who was part of your foundation died, but I knew having people around must help. But Faith hadn't even been able to look at me. I'd driven back to Vermont feeling miserable and like an idiot.

Cooper was right. I was an idiot. Still, he invited me to come see him after I did the obligatory holiday stuff with my families and promised a New Year's Eve party to blow my mind. I was pretty sure my mind would be ready for that.

Getting over Faith was going to be a long process. I'd tried it last year, so I knew this raw feeling would be around for a while. Talking to Faith about my hockey future had made some things very clear. I'd tried most of my life to earn attention and affection from my parents. It had never happened. It wasn't going to. I needed to make decisions for what was best for me. It sucked that it wasn't going to be something my parents would be happy about.

I could just add that to the things that were sucking in my life right now.

My parents' amicable divorce decreed that I was with my dad on Christmas Eve, then with my mom Christmas Day. As I'd grown up, I'd realized they hadn't been working out who would *get* to have me, but rather who would *have* to take me. It had been a stark and depressing realization.

So once school broke up for the holidays, I hung around on campus for a couple of extra days. That way, I could show up at my dad's in time for our Christmas Eve traditional "celebration" together without having that awkward period where they were busy with their lives and commitments and I'd have to hang around with nothing to do, just being in their way. At least at the hockey house I had a room that was only mine.

My parents lived a couple of hours apart. On Christmas morning, my dad would drive me to a prearranged meeting place about halfway between the two houses, and Mom would pick me up and drive me back to her place. After that, I'd hop on a plane to go see Cooper, to everyone's relief.

It would be great when I was done with school and was supporting myself. I'd have my own place, and I could send gifts and cards to my family and be where I was truly wanted for holidays.

During the handoff, we'd have a state of the union talk. Twice a year, when the parents were handing me over, we discussed the issues that concerned me and my future. There had been a time when the discussion was about which hockey camps I'd go to, and when I'd need to be dropped off and picked up. Once I was old enough to go on my own, it had been about arranging buses or trains and making sure I had the money I needed.

Nowadays, the meetings were short and sweet. Most of the time, I made suggestions and they signed off on them. Last summer, the exchange had been a little more serious and lengthier. They'd talked about hockey. That I should focus on my classes and getting my degree first. Hockey was great for providing the funding to get an education, but my degree should be the top priority. I'd nodded with them. It had been the most attention they'd paid me in...who knew how long. I'd felt like they'd seen me, were concerned about me. But I'd been fooling myself. I wasn't going to do that any longer.

Dad and I pulled into the service centre and sat at a table. He checked his watch before going to get us coffees. I knew they were waiting for him back at his home. I was, as usual, the holdup. For once, I wasn't going to feel guilty about it. I had a right to live, to have needs and wishes and dreams, and if that made things unpleasant for them, too fucking bad.

My mom came racing in. She was checking the time, too.

Could they just for once consider how I felt when they treated me like a damned hot potato?

"So how's school going?" my mom asked. They both smiled, pretending to care.

"Fine. Hockey's going even better."

They looked at each other. Yeah, they might not have had enough in common to stay married, but they both agreed on this. I wondered when they'd had a sit-down to discuss the problem of Sebastien, having to interact because of their "problem".

I wasn't a problem, and I was tired of feeling like one.

"That's nice, Sebastien, but like we discussed in the summer, your classes should be the first priority."

"With all due respect—" truthfully, I was debating how much was really due them, "—the two of you expressed your opinion that getting my degree and a regular job would be so much easier and less stressful for you. But I like hockey, and I'm good at it, and if that's my dream, I have every right to go for it. And that's what I've decided to do."

I couldn't blame them for looking shocked. I'd never pushed for what I wanted before. I hadn't had to do that for hockey, because they'd just been happy to send me away to a place where I wouldn't inconvenience them. I'd never asked for anything else for me. Never asked them to sacrifice beyond what they already did, since it was obviously such an issue for them.

I knew I had some fucked-up thinking in my head because of how I'd been raised. I didn't want to be defined by that, or to mess myself up because of it. This thing with Faith had made things all too clear. I'd thought what we'd had was the best thing ever, but it had been doomed by her parents' fuckups. I was not going to allow my parents' baggage to cause any more damage to my life.

I wish I could have done something to change the way things ended with Faith, but I could at least deal with my own shit. And this was the first step.

The state of the union went on longer than planned. There was something messed up about the fact that the most attention I'd ever gotten from my parents was coming when I was finally old enough to be considered an adult, and it was all because they were trying to ensure they didn't have to be responsible for me.

They didn't. I'd find my own people since they were too busy to be mine.

They both ended leaving the rest stop late enough to disrupt their Christmas dinners. I hadn't wanted to screw up anyone's holidays, but I was done feeling guilty. I'd put up with a lot over the years, trying to not be a burden, trying to make everyone else happy so they'd want me. I was done trying.

It was time to make me a priority.

19

Faith

It was going to be a horrible Christmas.

My dad's parents spent every winter in Florida, so they were never around for the holidays. They left gifts behind—usually cash—and always called before they went out golfing on the day. It was my mom's parents who'd been the centre of our Christmas celebrations. After Grandpa died, Gramma had continued that tradition. Last year, she hadn't been able to do much, but she'd been there, the heart of the holidays for us.

This year, she was gone.

My parents were fighting, though since it was Christmas, they were having a cold war. When they'd acted like this in the past, my grandmother had always made sure I was taken care of, made to feel special. Had someone paying attention to me. Now it was just me and my parents.

We opened presents on Christmas morning, and then my mom made a big production of how hard she was working to make the dinner. I offered to help, but she waved me off. The food was delicious, the conversation almost non-existent. Most of the time, I'd try to keep some kind of talk going, but I was out of fucks this year.

After Christmas, my dad hung around the house. He technically wasn't working over the holiday, unless a client got in a mess. He wanted to go to the rink and gym with me, help me train, talk hockey. I didn't want to talk about my problems with Coach with him because he'd stick himself in the middle, so those conversations were stilted. He was often distracted with phone calls, though, so we made it through.

My hockey success was largely because of him. He loved hockey, and I'd watched games with him as a kid. He'd taken me skating and signed me up for lessons. I was grateful for all he'd done when it came to hockey. He'd always made sure I had whatever I needed to succeed. He supported my dreams and wanted to be my agent when I turned pro. Only the family connection would be tricky, and my mom would see it as me taking his side, and I was not going to continue being in the middle of their fucked-up relationship.

My mom wanted me to help her clean out Gramma's place and choose what I wanted. I wasn't ready for that. I was still struggling to accept that she was gone, and as a college student living in a dorm, I wasn't really looking for family heirlooms to drag around. Plus, I knew Mom probably wanted to complain about Dad. After a couple of days of super uncomfortable juggling between the two of them, Dad got a call from one of his clients and had to jet. That should have made things easier, but not with my family.

My mom followed all my dad's clients on all forms of social media. So once Dad left, she started cyberstalking the client, their girlfriend...

It was depressing. This was why I was going to be single or find a nice accountant. Someone who stayed put, someone you could count on. Someone who wouldn't be surrounded by extra-relationship temptation and who could be trusted. If you couldn't trust your own father, who could you trust?

Sebastien

Getting to visit Cooper was a relief. Seeing the size of his home wasn't a surprise. I knew his family had money. Cooper had an older brother and an older sister, and they were all very busy, very important people. All lawyers or investment bankers or something money related like that. I wondered how a bunch of lawyers and bankers, apparently really successful ones, felt about Cooper playing hockey. He wanted to go pro. I knew he had declared a business major, and I'd never heard that he had problems keeping up his GPA, but outside of classes, he never showed interest in anything but hockey, girls, and parties.

I'd expected his family to feel about hockey the way mine did —that once you graduated, it was time to grow up and stop playing games. I never got a chance to find out how they felt, because I hardly saw them. They were always somewhere being busy and important.

Coop and I had a good time though. He had his own car, an Audi, not a Ferrari, so they were apparently wealthy but not to the point of buying a country. We did some working out, because Coach would have our balls in a vise if we got out of condition, but there was a lot of time to go to parties, and there were a lot of parties. Cooper knew everyone who hosted one, though he never had other people over to his place.

I didn't ask why that was. We all had our version of a fucked-up family.

I did my best to have fun. I thought I was pulling it off, until we headed out for the big New Year's bash Cooper had promised. I was wearing nice jeans, and Cooper had lent me a shirt to wear that he swore looked good on me. I didn't bother arguing with him, because based on the number of women who were always trying to get his attention, he knew what he was doing.

I did not.

"So, Hunts, you gonna have fun tonight or what?" It took a minute to figure out what he was saying, because my thoughts had been back on the Faith treadmill.

"What?" I'd hoped I'd fooled him.

"You said it's over with Faith, right?"

I nodded. It still hurt, but every time I went through what had happened, I was positive I'd done the right thing. She didn't trust me, would never trust me, and it would eventually end in disaster.

"So you're a free agent, right?"

I sighed. "Yeah, but it's not that easy. I can't just turn off what I felt."

"Can you at least try? This is your time, a chance to have fun. Don't piss it away." I thought Coop would tell me I was being stupid, which was probably fair, but instead, he was being reasonable.

I scrubbed my face with my hand, frustrated with myself. "I'm not pissing away anything. I'm having fun. I just need...a bit of time."

"Well, it's New Year's Eve. There are going to be a lot of single women at this party, so maybe you should consider if you've had enough time to at least kiss someone when the ball drops."

I was getting pissed with him, but I was pretty sure that's what he wanted. Maybe he thought it would kickstart me getting over Faith. "Are you seriously trying to get me angry enough to kiss someone just so I can shut you up?"

He flashed a grin at me. "Is it working?"

I had to laugh. "I'm not going to kiss someone just to prove something to you. But I'll try, okay? If something feels like it's working, I won't shut it down."

He punched the steering wheel. "That's all I want. There's a world of possibilities out there, Hunter. Keep your eyes open. I'm going to bring you to the fucking fun side yet."

"Maybe." I shot him a glance. "Maybe I'll bring you over to the relationship side."

"Right. You're making it look good right now."

He had a point. Breakups sucked. I needed to move on. After

all, I was the one who'd called it quits this time. But it wasn't because I didn't care about Faith.

If only it was that simple.

Faith

Getting back to school was a relief.

My dad hadn't returned, and my mom was still stalking his client. I'd tried again to tell her I was fine, and that she should leave Dad if she wanted to. I was on a scholarship, and I could take care of myself. She'd patted my cheek and said I didn't understand.

I didn't.

Back at school, I threw myself into hockey and classes. Coach asked if I was okay, and I assured her I was. I told her that being back here, keeping busy, was helping. Penny treated me like a wounded deer for the first couple of days, but finally she was convinced that I wasn't about to fall apart. Not again. The weather was cold, and we had a lot of snow, but I didn't mind. Back in Toronto, the snow always ended up gray and dingy. This was a smaller city, and things weren't as dirty. I liked it.

Playing hockey really belonged to cold weather. And playing where the world looked like a Christmas card was a bonus. I might as well enjoy what I could. We had a home stand, and I got one of the starts. I would have loved another shut out, but I let one in on a power play. We got the win though, and that was the important part.

The women's hockey house had a party after two wins that weekend. Fortunately, the men's team was snowed in at their away games, so I was able to go and forget about my problems. Or at least the one that played hockey.

I had fun. Not the kind of fun that would be on the highlight reel of my college life, but I managed to forget Seb and my family and enjoy being around people—people who weren't related to me or breaking up with me.

I could do this. I could be on my own and not worry about guys. If I wanted to hook up with someone, well, I was young. This was the time, right? I didn't want to hook up with anyone at this party. But that was my choice. When I felt like it, I would.

I drank a little more than I should, but there was no practice in the morning, and I was mostly caught up on schoolwork. I'd had lots of time to work on my reading while I was home over break. I slept in the day after the party and took some aspirin to get rid of the lingering effects. Penny wanted to go for brunch, and I was almost ready when my phone rang. It was my mom.

I didn't really want to answer. Her calls hadn't brought much good news this year. She was still on the outs with Dad, and she complained about him every time we talked. I'd told her she should leave him, but she wasn't going to, so the phone calls were just her excuse to vent. It always depressed me.

I knew she'd probably keep calling, so I answered, hoping it wasn't going to spoil my Sunday. I had decided though, that if she was going to tell me about some photo she'd seen of Dad, I was going to refuse to listen this time. She could leave him or not. That was her choice, but I didn't have to be part of it. Their relationship had messed with me, and it was time I set some limits.

That wasn't why she was calling though. Mom told me that Gramma had left her estate to us—to me and her. "That's great news, Mom."

I wasn't surprised, though she could have left everything to my mom. I didn't expect much beyond the furniture and silverware that my mom had been trying to get me to choose while we cleaned up Gramma's apartment. But Gramma had more. It wasn't a fortune, not millions, but there was a lot more than anyone had known about. Two thirds were going to my mom, and one third to me. The money I was getting would easily handle the cost of school for as long as I needed or could pay for a house.

Although maybe not much of a house in Toronto. This meant my mom had a lot coming to her.

She wanted to know what I was going to do with my money. The money I hadn't even known I was going to get until five minutes ago.

"It'll take a while to go through probate, Mom, but I'm good for now. I don't know. I'll just invest it or something until I need it. What about you?"

Mom started listing options—a vacation place, or something like that, and then it hit me. She could leave Dad. She didn't have to stay and be miserable and humiliated. She could get her own place, divorce Dad, and do anything she wanted.

She'd stayed for years because of me and money and who knows what else. But I was gone, for all intents and purposes. With this inheritance, I wouldn't need to live at home again. Mom had enough money to enjoy herself. Maybe she could even find someone who wouldn't cheat on her. I knew it would take some convincing though. She'd been stuck for so long.

"Hey, Mom, why don't you get your own place?"

The silence was deafening.

"I mean, you say how unhappy Dad makes you." Our last call had been mostly about that. "Now you can move out. I'm taken care of, so you can just worry about you."

Maybe I was being disloyal to Dad, but surely he'd be happier, too? I mean, he was always cheating, so he couldn't be happy, right?

"Faith, you don't know what you're talking about."

"I know I've never been married, Mom, or had kids, but I grew up in that house. I know you're not happy because you tell me that. I know you wanted things to be good for me, and you were worried about money, but now you don't have to be. You can do anything you want."

"I know that. And I do the things I want to."

She'd complained about Dad for years. They fought. Over and over. What the hell was she talking about?

"You are still a child and don't know anything."

She'd complained to me most of my life. I did know something. "I know that every time Dad goes out of town, you stalk him online. I know that you've complained about his cheating for years. I know you've told me you can't leave him because of me and money and whatever else. Well, I'm gone, and you have money."

"Faith, you're distraught. We'll talk later."

She hung up on me. She fucking hung up on me. It made me angry. I wanted to hit something. I couldn't stay still. I told Penny I needed to cancel brunch, put on running gear and my shoes, and went for a run.

I knew I was just her daughter, and I didn't know all about marriage, but she'd made me aware of their problems because she fucking complained all the time. And now, when she finally had a chance to start over, she was going to stay with Dad, try to catch him cheating, have a big fight, and do it all over again? How sick was that? It was totally sick. And twisted. And I refused to be part of it anymore. If she was going to do that, I was not going to listen. I was not going to be part of it. I was not going to be like my damned mother and live that life.

I would've liked to talk about it with someone, but I wasn't comfortable enough with Penny to talk about Mom and Dad. I had to be careful around athletes, because my dad worked with them. If Seb—

That thought just pushed me to run harder.

I was sweaty when I got back to my room. Penny had gone for brunch without me, but she was back now. She wanted to show me some pictures of what I'd missed, but I needed to shower first.

I apologized for bailing on her. She told me it was probably just as well I hadn't gone. Some of the guys from the hockey team had been there, and Seb, too.

A part of me curled up into a tiny ball. I wondered if he'd been there with someone.

Penny showed the incredible waffles she'd had but then

quickly closed out of the app. I drew in a long breath. I understood why. I didn't really want her to know how much I wondered about Seb, about what he was doing, and who he was doing it with.

I could look on my own—

Boom. It was like a puck to the head. I could stalk him online...just like my mother. I could live in a world of suspicion and jealousy...just like my mother. In fact, that was exactly what I was doing. When I didn't get a message from Seb, I'd looked him up online. I'd *expected* to find him cheating and had immediately interpreted that picture that way.

I'd learned that behavior from my mother.

I'd confronted him, waiting for him to give an explanation that I would tear apart. I would've waited for the next time, the next picture, when he might not have had an explanation that I couldn't tear apart.

Just like Mom.

I was my mother. And I'd destroyed my relationship with the best guy I'd ever meet, because *I was my mother*.

How the hell could I feel superior to her when I was doing the same damn thing?

20

Sebastien

We were back in the routine of school and games again. I loved it. It was better to be here with my teammates and friends than carefully skirting the outside of my parents' lives. They weren't happy with me and were showing their displeasure by not speaking to me. That was after they'd tried to blame each other for my decision.

I was old enough now to be on my own and make my own decisions, and it looked like that meant being nothing but acquaintances with them from now on. That hurt. Not like we'd been close before, but I'd hoped things would one day be different.

Still, I felt lighter. I didn't have to bear the weight of their expectations anymore. I could do what I wanted, or needed, without having to feel guilty. We'd have to discuss what was going to happen this summer, but I could make that decision for me. I didn't have to talk them into it. I'd tell them what I was doing, and they could decide how to respond.

I'd probably need to get a job. I'd speak to Coach to see if he knew of anything. It was a little scary, but I mostly felt good.

About classes, and hockey, and taking charge of my life. There was also the Faith issue. I still missed her. Not just the few weeks we'd been together here at school. We'd been together for almost two years before that stupid non-cheating thing last year. We worked together so well. I didn't want to be without her.

I'd rethought my decision over and over. I could go back to her, tell her about Marcher and Raylene, explain that nothing had happened. It was tempting. Except I knew it would happen again. And I couldn't control the pictures that were posted or the stories that would be written. If I was lucky enough to get drafted and play professionally, it was going to be worse.

The thought of never knowing if Faith would be happy to see me or be like she had that day, closed off, waiting for the blow... I couldn't always be wondering if there'd be something that would destroy her faith in me, giving her a reason to leave. Never knowing or being in control of that made my stomach roil. I deserved someone who would love me. Stay with me. Someone who would at least give me the benefit of the doubt. I didn't think that person could ever be Faith, as much as I'd love it to be.

I hadn't kissed anyone on New Years. I'd planned to. But about five minutes before the countdown, I chickened out. I'd gone to find a bathroom and hid out there until the big celebration was over.

Now, a couple of weeks into the new semester, I was tired. Tired of looking for Faith in order to avoid her. Tired of arguing this over and over in my head. It was enough. Hanging on to someone who'd never believe in me wasn't something I needed in my life. I'd already gotten enough of that from my parents.

Last year, I'd dated, but I'd never been all in. I realized that now, and it hadn't been fair to those girls. Like Holly. I'd picked girls who weren't like Faith on purpose, which meant that I hadn't been over her. I'd been ready to be a good boyfriend, but I'd never risked getting too involved. It was time to get over that.

Maybe I should try being more like Cooper and like a lot of

my teammates. Pick up girls, have a fun hookup, leave them behind. Maybe. I wasn't sure that was something I could do. But what I could do was move on. I had a lot of life left, I hoped. I needed to find someone who could know and love the real me, so I needed to show who I was.

I was going to go to the next party we had and be open to possibilities. Whether it was some hot sex, a blow job, or just some ego-stroking flirtation would depend on who was there and how I felt, but I was going to try, damn it. I should feel a little happier about it than I did right now, but I would. Fake it 'til you make it, right?

I headed down to the kitchen and saw Cooper was dressed up. Well, he was wearing jeans and not sweats.

"Are you going out?"

He cocked his head. "Yeah, party at the basketball players' house tonight."

"Can I come with?"

He stared at me, a frown creasing his face. "You sure about that?"

I stared back at him. "Yeah, I am."

He watched me for another minute and then shrugged. "Sure. Are we avoiding anyone tonight?"

I shook my head. "No, we're just looking for fun."

Cooper smirked. "Welcome to the dark side, padawan."

Faith

The revelation that I was behaving like my mom had hit me hard. It was absolutely the last thing I wanted to be, but once I looked at my own behavior, really looked at it, it was impossible to miss.

I wanted to find Seb immediately. I wanted to tell him I was sorry, and that I got it now. It was my fault, but I'd change. I could change, couldn't I? Or was this too ingrained by now? That thought terrified me. I couldn't live like that. Unless I planned to live alone. And I didn't want to do that.

What I wanted was what I'd had with Seb. Someone who believed in me, helped me when I needed, held me when all that I wanted was comfort. Someone who made me feel sexy and attractive, and someone who could almost blind me with excellent orgasms. That's what I'd had with Seb, and that's what I wanted back.

I had to be sure I could commit to changing before I talked to him. I'd been raised all my life in an atmosphere of suspicion. I had to learn how to have faith be more than just my name.

This wasn't like other goals I'd set for myself. I couldn't increase the number of reps or laps or stretches I did to improve my fitness, take more shots, watch more game tape. It wasn't even like homework. I wasn't sure exactly what it was, but I had to figure it out. I had to learn to trust Seb.

I gave myself two weeks. I was going to have two weeks of not checking on Seb, not looking for any evidence of what he was doing. I needed to cut myself off from those behavior patterns. I needed to spend some time on my own, weeding out all the things I'd taken on without thinking.

I did a lot of running, thinking about what it would be like to really trust someone. I got really tired and wore out a pair of shoes. I put an elastic on my wrist, like people quitting smoking did. And whenever I recognized thought patterns about what Seb could be doing, or anything negative related to that, I'd snap the elastic. I broke a couple of them the first week. But it started to work. I found my thoughts diverting even before I snapped my wrist.

While I was going through this self-examination time, I decided to talk to my coach. I'd had another weekend of not suiting up. We'd lost a couple of games I honestly thought I could have made a difference in. Coach wanted team players. And I was one. I had to figure out how to prove it to her. I'd tried the easier way for me by playing well, but that wasn't enough.

I had to talk to Coach, to try to explain, and then I'd know I'd done my best. I went to her office after practice and knocked on the doorframe.

"What is it, Devereaux?" Coach was behind her desk, a guarded look on her face. She had to know why I wanted this private chat. She didn't look thrilled at the prospect.

I swallowed. "Can I talk to you for a couple of minutes?"

Coach sighed, like this was an imposition, but she nodded, and I sat in the chair across from her. There was a moment of silence, and then I decided to spill. There wasn't a lot to lose.

"I played on my first all-female team two years ago."

She was watching me over crossed arms. "Because you couldn't play on the boys' teams anymore."

My hands tensed on the chair. "Exactly. I didn't get to choose whether I wanted to play with women or men. That choice was taken away from me. I couldn't choose because I didn't have a dick between my legs."

Coach's eyebrows rose.

"My dad had always put me on co-ed teams, and later, he fought to get me on boys' teams because he wanted me to be the best. I never got much choice about who I played with then, either."

I hadn't minded. I'd liked playing with the guys, learning with them. I'd been comfortable with them, but I hadn't considered there were other options.

"I like this team. This women's team. I like having locker rooms where I'm one of the group, not shuffled off into a storage room because I'm different. I like that I don't have to pretend I never have a period because then I'm not one of the guys. I like playing with people who have the same basic body as me so we can talk about bras and chafing and things I never could talk about with the guys."

Coach's arms were uncrossed now, but her expression was still skeptical.

"I like it, but I hate that I couldn't choose. And I want to play on men's teams to show that I can be better than they are, that I'm tougher, and so that one day, if I have a daughter, she won't have her choice taken away. I want to be on this team. It's a good team, and I want to bring a championship here for the women. I also want the men's team to know that we're not second rate or second class just because we have vaginas."

I drew a breath and mentally adjusted my big-girl panties. "I'd like my coach to help me with that." I let out a breath and looked at the ground. "So, um, that's what I wanted to say." I stood, ready to go.

"Sit down," she snapped.

I sat, wondering if I'd just detonated my college hockey career and everything that followed.

Coach leaned forward across her desk. "I know that took guts to say. We may have gotten started on the wrong foot. I've had to fight for everything for the women's team here, while the men's team are gifted things without even asking. I'm a big proponent of women's sports, and I'm sensitive about any perceived disrespect. If you're committed a hundred percent to this team, then I want you here. You're a damn good player. But your father isn't going to have a say in what I do. And I don't want anyone on my team who signed up just looking to score a hockey player."

I looked her in the eyes. "I don't want my father to have a say in what I do, either, so if he's been talking to you, that wasn't anything I asked for."

The next comment required more courage. "I have never used my sport or my team to try to get a guy. I think I've lost my shot with my hockey player, but I'll warn you, I'm going to try to get him back. Not that my first choice is an athlete, because our schedules are brutal, but…" I shrugged. There was no one else as good for me. No one else I was in love with.

Coach finally cracked a smile. "I've seen how you play. If you use that same focus on him, he's in trouble."

I counted down until my two weeks were up. It wasn't easy.

Without the anger and suspicion to distract me, I'd missed Seb. Part of it was the sex, because that was great. But it was so much more than that. I wanted to tell him about talking to Coach, and how we'd cleared the air. It was exactly what he'd told me to do. I wanted to sit and study with him, watch him rub his eyebrows with his finger when he was absorbed in what he was reading. I wanted to hear that grunt in his throat when something surprised him. I wanted to talk hockey with him and ask what he'd decided about the draft and his family.

I really wanted to see the flush in his cheeks and those half-mast eyes when he was close to coming. When he couldn't say anything beyond, "Fuck, fuck, fuck," because there was no blood left in his brain. I wanted to hear that breathless, helpless moan when he came and then was boneless around me. I needed to rein in those thoughts, because they made me want things that I wasn't sure I'd ever have again. I missed him. I hoped he'd believe me when I said I'd changed. That I would try.

It had been difficult to wait, but I had to have something to show him that would convince him it was worth taking another chance on me. I'd wanted to check social media or hang around the arena to see him and who he might be with. Once, I'd given Penny my phone for a night because I didn't trust myself. Trust did not come easily. I'd worked and practiced for everything else in my life, and I would apply that to this as well.

The hockey house finally had another party happening. It was someone's birthday. I didn't care who. I only had one reason to go to the party. Penny helped me get ready, so I was looking the best I could. She'd promised to come as support, but I'd thanked her and told her I needed to do this on my own.

She lent me her lucky scarf. It reminded me of Seb. I gave her a hug, tight and sincere. Some things had gone badly this year, but I'd lucked out with my roommate. Penny hugged me back, told me I was going to get my man, and watched me head down the hallway like it was the first day of school, and I was her kid. I'd been less nervous then.

If I'd lost Seb, if I couldn't convince him to give us another try, I was going to hurt badly.

Even though it was January and cold, there were people hanging out on the porch, and a couple of the windows were open. Condensation on the glass showed it was warm inside. I greeted a couple of the guys I knew and saw Zoe, one of my teammates. I waved at her, but I had one objective, and I didn't let myself be distracted.

I made it into the house. The place was crowded, packed wall to wall. As one of the taller girls, I normally had a good chance to find someone in a crowd, but this party had a lot of really tall guys. I was pretty sure I saw some basketball players, so I didn't have much chance to look over their heads.

Someone offered me a cup of something, probably beer, and I shook my head. I wasn't stupid enough to drink anything I hadn't acquired from a trusted source, and I needed a clear head tonight. I worked my way around bodies, but I didn't see Seb in the front room, so I twisted my way through to the kitchen where people were helping themselves to a keg. I finally found him in the next room, where a game of beer pong was going on.

I hadn't seen him since the funeral, and that had been a haze. The time before that, he'd been walking away because I couldn't trust him. It had been a long time, maybe too long. It was ridiculous the way my breathing was tight and shallow. My stomach had wound into a ball, and my hands and feet were cold even though I could feel sweat starting to drip down my back and breastbone. I took a long, calming breath.

Cooper was there beside him, which wasn't unexpected. There were also girls, which was typical of these parties at the hockey house. There was a girl with a hand around Seb's arm. A blonde this time, very pretty, and obviously very interested in Seb.

Spots blurred my vision and I felt dizzy. I reached a hand out to the wall. Waiting so long had been a risk I'd taken because I'd wanted to have something to offer him. I had no ties on him. He was free to find someone else.

He wasn't cheating, but he was going to break my heart.

21

Faith

I wanted to run, turn and escape from this place. I wanted to
have quiet and privacy to work through the pain, because I knew
there would be a lot of crying, but not yet. I wasn't going to do it
like this, not anymore. I was determined that I wasn't going to
decide what was happening based on a quick impression. I wasn't
going to assume Seb would cheat on me based on a photo, and I
wouldn't assume I'd lost him because a girl had her hand
wrapped around his arm. I was going to take the pain, wait for
the truth, and deal with facts, not suspicions and interpretations.

I was going to be an adult even if it killed me, and right now, it
kinda felt like it would.

I was also going to get a beer, because there were limits to
what I could take without the edges smoothed off. It gave me a
respite before I had to look and see that girl with Seb again. I took
one of the empty cups and waited for my turn at the keg. I braced
myself mentally, because when that beer was done, I'd go and
watch to see if Seb had found someone easier. Someone less
messed up.

Someone who wasn't me.

"Faith?"

My hand shook around my cup. Seb was there behind me, saying my name. I swallowed, preparing myself to find him holding the blonde close. Prepared to find out he had a new girlfriend. Prepared to face facts.

I didn't bother with a smile as I turned. It was going to look wrong anyway, with the edges slipping away as I tried not to cry. He was standing there looking so damned good, and he was alone. I didn't know where the blonde was. She might still be Seb's new girlfriend. She wasn't here now, though, and I had something to say, something Seb deserved to hear.

"Seb, can we talk? Outside? I just need a minute." It was too loud in here for the apology I owed him.

"You okay?"

I nodded and headed for the front door.

The porch was empty now since the temperature had dropped some more. This should be a short conversation. I turned, leaning against the post for support. I was still holding the stupid cup, but it was empty. I was going to talk to him completely sober.

Seb stood a couple of feet away from me, waiting. His face was mostly in shadow. I took a minute to gather my thoughts, but I needed to do this, and I wasn't going to put it off.

"I want to apologize. I wasn't fair to you. I kept looking for ways you were like my dad instead of seeing the person you really are. I was waiting for you to cheat instead of appreciating that you aren't like that, and I'm sorry I implied you are. I projected my own problems on to you, and you didn't deserve that."

He was watching me, but I couldn't make out his features in the dark. I thought that might be better. Easier.

I went on. "I'm sorry I lost you, and I wish you all the best. You'll make someone a great boyfriend. I only wish it was with me. Not every girl out there just sees you as a hockey player. You're a good guy, and they can see that." I didn't think my voice was going to last much longer, but I'd gotten it out there. I looked around and then held the empty cup out to Seb.

"I'm gonna go now, so…"

Seb grabbed my wrist instead of the cup. "Wait, Faith. What are you saying?"

I had hoped I'd been clear. With his warm hand on my wrist, it was hard to remember exactly what words I'd used now. "I was wrong. You were right. I can't jump to conclusions. I have to trust you, and I didn't do that. It wasn't fair to you, and I'm sorry."

He tugged me closer. I couldn't resist. Closer to Seb was exactly where I wanted to be.

"Can you do that?" His voice was low, a little gruff. "Will you?"

I looked up into his intent brown eyes. "What?"

It was hard to think this close to him. All I wanted to do was touch him, kiss him.

"Can you trust me?"

I swallowed. "I gave myself a test. I didn't check for anything about you online for two weeks. I decided I had to let that go. But—"

"But what?"

I closed my eyes, not quite brave enough to see his face when I repeated this. "But if you've found someone else, that's okay."

There was a pause, and I finally had to look at him.

Seb shook his head. "It's not okay. And I haven't."

I blinked at him. I wanted to ask about that girl, the blonde I saw him with, but I didn't. He'd been standing by a girl. She'd touched him. He hadn't touched her, and he said he hadn't found someone. I was going to trust that.

"You haven't?"

"It's not that easy to get over you, Faith. Believe me, I've tried."

He didn't sound exactly happy about that, but I was kind of glad he hadn't. I'd tried to get over him as well, but… "I know. I mean, I tried, too."

Seb tugged me tightly against him, and it felt so damn good.

"You sure about this, Faith?"

"I'm not even sure what we're talking about." I had my head resting on his shoulder, and I was breathing in his familiar smell and finding it difficult to focus on words. Damn, I'd missed him.

"You. Me. Trust."

Right. We had to work this out or no snuggling, no smelling, no kissing, no Seb. I straightened upright. "I'd like it if there was a you and me again. And if I don't trust you, I'll deal with it, I promise. I can go for a run, or—"

Seb put a finger on my lips. "No, if you have a problem, you talk to me. But you have to believe what I tell you."

I nodded. "Okay." I whispered the word against his finger, and he let it drop.

"What about that girl in there?"

Damn it, I'd promised myself I wouldn't do this. But he said to talk to him. So I was.

Seb frowned and looked back. "There were a lot of girls in there."

"A blonde. She had her hand on your arm by the beer pong table. I thought maybe—"

Seb shook his head, wariness in his gaze. "I'm not sure of her name. Never met her before, as far as I know."

This was it. I could trust him, take that as given, or I could decide he was lying, or try to track the girl down. I needed the elastic on my wrist.

I closed my eyes and took a deep breath. "Okay, I believe you. But if she puts her hands on you again..." I could take her. Absolutely.

Seb took a step back. "What if she does? What if I come out after a game, and people want pictures with me, and they put their hands on me?"

I raised my chin, still meeting his gaze. "I'll trust you. But if someone does it while I'm there, I might not be responsible for what I'll do..."

Seb brushed my cheek with his fingers. "Faith, I love you. It's only ever been you. If you have doubts, just tell me."

I would. I could. I'd do this. I nodded. "And then what?"

A slow smile stretched across his face, and his eyes were heated. We'd somehow pulled close again, and I could see his expression clearly.

"Then I'll have to take you to my room and do bad, bad things to you until you don't doubt me anymore."

I chewed on my lip while I considered that. "For a psych major, you don't seem to understand motivation very well."

"Now, if I find guys coming on to you—"

"Me?"

"I'm going to have to take you to your room and do bad, bad things until you don't let them do that."

Huh. I hadn't considered that Seb might be jealous. But I liked this playful side to him, and I wondered if he'd never felt confident enough to be that way before. Because of me. I was going to make it up to him. And I had some very good ideas about how to do it. None of them were appropriate for the front porch of the hockey house.

"It sounds like there's going to be a lot of sex in my future." I couldn't sound upset about that if I tried.

Seb rested his forehead against mine. "You got a problem with that?"

I shook my head. "But, um, what if I need a little reassurance now?"

Seb grinned. "I guess I'm just going to have to get very, very bad."

I grinned back at him. "Well, if that's what it takes…"

EPILOGUE

Sebastien

It was too late for a toddler to be up, but this was a special night. It wasn't every day that a girl's mom was going to achieve her lifelong dream and make history. Hailey and I were in the owner's box for the Toronto Blaze. I'd watched a few games here, ever since I'd started working for the organization rather than playing for them. I'd been drafted by Toronto and enjoyed being part of the on-ice team here for a couple of years, but a serious concussion had moved me off the ice.

Faith had been pregnant at the time, and I did not want to risk any time with my family, so rather than risk another knock on the head, I'd retired. The Blaze, being the quality hockey club that they were, had given me a job with the team. We'd been able to keep our place near the arena and didn't have to juggle two different cities to be a family. Together, we managed to care for Hailey, our daughter.

And now, Faith's dream was coming true.

It was too bad her family hadn't been able to make it for the game, but this had been a last-minute, crazy thing that had just blown up. The kind that didn't seem real, or possible, until it actually happened. The Blaze's starting goalie had appendicitis, and his backup got caught in a pileup in practice and sprained his ankle. He'd come close to snapping the bone, and the tendons were seriously stretched, so the team didn't want him putting that swollen joint in a skate.

That meant calling up a goalie from the minors, someone who could make it in time to pull on their gear. They'd called someone on their emergency list to be the backup goalie for the game.

Faith Devereaux.

Faith played for the Toronto Blaze's women's team, and we lived close to the arena, so there was no problem getting here even at this last minute. When Faith got the phone call, I'd thought someone was seriously ill. She'd frozen, shocked. Then she'd almost screamed the place down. It was the news she'd been waiting for almost her whole life.

She'd dressed for an NHL game and was now on the bench. She wasn't used to being the backup, not anymore. She was the starter for her team and had been for years. We'd planned Hailey around Faith's hockey season, so she'd missed as little ice time as possible.

This evening had already been a big, newsworthy event. And having Faith as the official backup goalie for a regular season game was ground-breaking. I'd been given a heads-up that the team was ready to make more headlines. We were almost at the end of the second intermission, and even through Hailey was flagging, we weren't leaving.

Toronto was up a goal. The minor league guy was doing a good job, and the team's defense had been making sure he wasn't tested too badly. But the Blaze were a great organization, and they knew how to work a moment like this.

I had my eyes glued on Faith when the team came out for the third period. And even though I couldn't see her face, I knew the moment they'd sprung the news on her.

They were putting her in net for the third.

It was happening. She was playing in a real, regular-season, meaningful game. A woman.

She turned, looking up at the box where she knew I'd be. I was grinning ear to ear and held up Hailey. Faith wouldn't be able to see, but Hailey had a Blaze jersey with Faith's name and number on it, same as me. Not sure how the team had gotten them done that quickly, but they had, and everyone in the box had one on.

I watched her skate to her net, do her starting maneuvers, and set into her position, ready to play, ready to win. I'd never thought we'd get here after that terrible misunderstanding, and with the shitty stuff our families put us through, but we'd had our second chance, a second half. And we'd made it work.

The puck dropped. My wife deflected the first shot on goal. My daughter and I cheered.

It was perfect.

THE
END

ACKNOWLEDGMENTS

When Sarina Bowen announced that she was opening up her True North world to other authors, I was excited to apply and shocked when my story, Halftime, was approved! Getting to write in the Moo U hockey universe, after reading everything Sarina has written, was incredible. Writing a series covering four seasons of hockey and with so many talented authors was a challenge involving a lot of sharing and spreadsheets. It's been an incomparable learning opportunity, and I thank Sarina, Jane, Jenn and all the other authors for their generosity and support. Thanks to Heidi Shoham for her editing services, and my Pitsquirrels for reading, commenting, supporting, and encouraging. Thanks to my husband for his patience in what has been a hectic writing year. I hope you enjoy following the journey of Faith and Seb as much as I have.